the

POWER

of

COLOR

the POWER of COLOR

Dr. Morton Walker

AVERY PUBLISHING GROUP INC.

Garden City Park, New York

This book has been written and published strictly for informational purposes, and in no way should it be used as a substitute for recommendations from your own medical doctor or health care professional. All the facts included come from medical files, clinical journals, scientific publications, personal interviews, published trade books, self-published materials by experts in the field, magazine articles, and the personal-practice experiences of the authorities quoted or sources cited. You should not consider educational material found here to be the practice of medicine or to replace consultation with a physician or other medical practitioner. Dr. Morton Walker and his publisher are providing you with the information in this work so that you can have the understanding, and choose the option to act on that understanding, at your own risk.

Cover design: Rudy Shur and Janine Eisner-Wall
Cover photo credit: The Stock Market © 1989 Al Francekevich
In-house editor: Elaine Will Sparber

The McGraw-Hill dictionary definition on page 1 is reproduced with permission of McGraw-Hill, Inc. It is from the *McGraw-Hill Dictionary of Scientific and Technical Terms*, 4th Edition © 1989 by McGraw-Hill.

The Doubleday dictionary definition on page 1 is reprinted with permission from *The Doubleday Dictionary for Home, School, and Office* © 1975 by Doubleday.

Library of Congress Cataloging-in-Publication Data

Walker, Morton.
  The power of color : the art and science of making colors work for you / Morton Walker.
     p. cm.
  Includes bibliographical references (p. 169) and index.
  ISBN 0-89529-430-3
  1. Color—Psychological aspects. 2. Color—Therapeutic use.
  I. Title
  BF789.C7W35 1991
  152.14'5—dc20   90-19501
                                                               CIP

Contents

To Lisa and Michael,
two of the most colorful little people I know.

Foreword

Reading *The Power of Color,* by Morton Walker, D.P.M., was a distinct pleasure for me. Colour therapy (healing with colour) and chromatology (the science of colour) are among my special medical interests.

I had the inexpressible satisfaction of realizing that the results of scientific investigations on colour conducted over the years by my medical team and me are already well accepted in the United States of America—a far distance from my own locality here in Athens, Greece.

For decades, Europeans have researched colour's nature and the important role it plays in the field of medicine in both the prevention and treatment of illness for all human beings. Representing my fellow scientists at the Medical Institute for Homoeopathic Research and Application, an international organization, I declare that Dr. Walker has written a highly readable, fully documented, and truly scientific treatise on the power of colour to heal pathology, maintain homoeostasis, influence decision-making, affect psychology, impel emotions, persuade purchasing, and predispose people to perform in all manner of behaviour. He has confirmed the studious conclusions reached by scientists worldwide, whom he frequently mentions, often has interviewed, and invariably quotes in this lucid and easily understood book. This book is a superb representation of his work and deserves acclaim not only in his own country, but also by the world.

Dr. Morton Walker, of Stamford, Connecticut, has produced a capturing presentation on colour. He reveals step-by-step in a conceivable way what a powerful tool colour is if properly applied in health care, psychology, nutrition, home decorating, the workplace environment, sociology, and marketing. Combining the investigative talents of a science reporter, the writing skill of a medical journalist, and the physiological background acquired from his training and former practice as a doctor of podiatric medicine, Dr. Walker has succeeded in classifying, examining, and presenting scientific proofs on the nature and function of colour in our lives. His proofs and analyses are derived from a great variety of sources that if regarded with an open mind will teach the reader how to utilize the tremendously positive impact of colour in his personal and professional life and evolution.

Colour has today become one of the most basic characteristics of our lives. Great technological advances have let us create thousands of chromatic shades, which dominate our daily visual environment and bombard us with thousands of stimuli that are classified in our brains. Colour thus signifies the beginning of physical and psychological reactions and functions. To employ colour correctly and to the most benefit, we need a scientific approach. We can find that science laid out for us right here in *The Power of Color*.

Chromatics, the term I have adopted for the science of colour, has proved a coloured light beam—especially a monochromatic one—carries energy that is transmitted to man when he comes into contact with it. I arrived at this conclusion after twenty years of research. Energy properties characterizing the colour and stored within it are offered to man for his use and benefit. Dr. Walker also has reached and extensively analyzed this basic conclusion, and I am grateful. He came to his same conclusion by vast literature searches, interviews with those on the cutting edge of colour therapy, and evaluation of methods of marketing, selling, merchandizing, advertising, etc. And he explains these many concepts ever so clearly in the engrossing chapters of this fabulous book. The inquiring mind will find this book all-inclusive on colour—a page-turner. It is packed with information for all of us to enjoy and usefully employ.

A fine correlation between colour and sound energy is presented here, along with the intricate and fascinating phenomenon of aura. Equally intriguing is the vast amount of information about the effects of colour on purchasing decisions and other related aspects of daily living. Read on, for you will learn why, when, from whom, and how you buy things that you may or may not really want!

There is a special relationship between certain colours and the individual. Why someone prefers or detests a certain shade or tone has to do with both the properties inherent in that colour plus the person's energy status at the moment. For instance, if you have ever tried to relax in a room painted red, then you may recall the uncomfortable feeling you experienced. Even after closing your eyes, you probably could not relax. This emotional irritation is explained by the basic quality of red that creates a disposition for action. The colour red also creates a desire for communicating, gives energy, warms, increases vitality, and releases suppressed energy. Dr. Walker tells you a lot more about red, and about the many other colours as well.

In order to make correct choices in colour use, you must learn the various qualities of the colours of the visible spectrum. Those choices will improve or detract from the quality of life. Educating you this way is Dr. Walker's forte; he is expert as an emancipator of thought, educator of fact, writer of occurrence, and verbal communicator of results achieved. By means of the written word especially, as in *The Power of Color*, this author succeeds with the greatest efficacy.

In the main part of his book, Dr. Walker refers to colour therapy or "chromotherapy." Here, colour is described as a mild yet very powerful form of energy that can be employed to restore an individual's daily energy losses. It is likely the diligent use of colour can help a person overcome chronic fatigue syndrome and other such energy-reducing disorders.

Currently in health care around the world—including in Dr. Walker's country, the United States, and in mine, Greece—we have reached a point where the individual must take a more active role concerning his state of wellness. Chromotherapy will aid a person in doing just that. It has numerous applications, no side effects, and is based on easily comprehensible principles. These facts make it an ideal method for the relief of several common ailments, but you must apply the knowledge.

The knowledge afforded by *The Power of Color* need not only be administered as therapy, but can also be included in the field of prevention. As a medical doctor and administering colour therapist who accepts the task of facing patients in pain daily in my clinical practice, I believe that as more people are properly educated in matters relating to their health, the battles against disease and pain will be more easily won.

A book about the power of colour such as this one written by Dr. Morton Walker—who is highly regarded as a medical journalist and considered with the greatest respect internationally by exponents of complementary medicine, wholistic medicine, orthomolecular nutrition, and alternative methods of healing—is another significant advancement in the understanding of phenomena in our world. This book combines the best of Eastern medicine, Western traditionalist science, New Age thinking, the spiritual aspects of life, and incomprehensible mysticism.

As I stated before, *The Power of Color* asks the reader to have an open mind. It is presented responsibly, brings scientific information to the public, and offers immense help to suffering humanity. My sincere wish and fond desire is that it meets with the well-received response from consumers and scientists alike that it truly deserves.

Professor Dr. Spiro Diamantidis, M.D., M.A.,
color therapist and chromatologist,
president, Medical Institute for
Homoeopathic Research and Application
Athens, Greece

Preface

Did you know that if a person with hypertension swims in a blue swimming pool, his elevated blood pressure temporarily lowers?

Did you know that red pepper fed to chickens makes the yolks of their eggs red?

Did you know that if a person wears red socks all day, he goes to bed with warm feet, but if he wears black socks, he goes to bed with cold feet?

Did you know that colors cue shoppers to buy certain brands or categories of products? For example, Coca-Cola owns red in the soft drink arena. The Berni Company, image-makers for sugar-free Canada Dry ginger ale, contends that after it changed the ginger ale can from red (which communicates a cola message) to green and white (which communicates a message of flavor but not cola), sales of Canada Dry ginger ale surged 27 percent within six months.

Did you know that blue (connoting slimness) is associated with club soda, low-calorie skim milk, and cottage cheese; green (interpreted as life-giving) is connected with vegetables and chewing gum?

Did you know that green is a poor color in which to package pastry or meats because it tends to remind potential purchasers of the furry coating formed by fungus, yeast, and mold?

Did you know that a package with earth tones such as brown, tan, dark orange, and golden yellow indicates to consumers a natural, preservative-free product?

Did you know that pastries from a pink box seem to taste better than pastries coming from a box of any other color?

Davis Masten, chairman of the image-consulting firm of Cheskin and Masten, says that marketers and some other professionals need to be intuitively clever in harnessing the psychological power of colors. For instance, engineers paint bridges blue when they stretch high over water or chasms to restrain potential suicides from jumping. Blue has a sedating effect. Moreover, when architects changed schoolroom walls from orange and white to blue, students' blood pressure dropped and their behavior and learning comprehension soared.

Carlton Wagner, head of the Wagner Institute for Color Research in Santa Barbara, California, distributed four different multicolored cardboard soapboxes at various laundromats in twelve test markets in March 1989. Each of the boxes contained exactly the same detergent, but the consumers tested felt neutral about the soap powder in the green-and-white and orange-and-green boxes, questioned whether the mild powder in the blue-and-white carton even contained any soap, and declared the detergent in the orange-and-blue box to be "super potent." One consumer even thought the soap powder in the last box was strong enough to take the tar stains off his automobile's damaged fender. Wagner was not surprised at the strong illusion—a kind of placebo effect—given by this particular orange-and-blue soapbox. Blue, he contends, connotes authority and commands respect; orange suggests power and affordability. Thus, people reacted to the soap according to the color of the soapbox.

Did you know that wearing white and other light colors helps overweight people reduce their caloric intake? White clothing makes a person appear heavier.

Did you know that because of its vast expenditures to trademark its blue color image, the International Business Machines Corporation (IBM) holds the unwritten title to blue in the corporate category?

Did you know that colors affect a person's well-being? They can bring on illness or promote wellness. When someone wishes to tune the body to the finer forces in life—for instance, the physiological forces that intricately quicken or slow the pulse rate, increase or decrease the volume of blood flow, and even stimulate or cease blood clotting—he can use one of the most wonderful therapies available in the healing arts. Although organized allopathic medicine as generally practiced in the United States has not yet discovered the therapeutic effects of color, assuredly it's color that creates these phenomena in mankind! Yes, the body, mind, and mood all mold themselves internally and externally to color the same as they do to food.

Color is a form of food. "Light is a nutrient, and, like food, is necessary for optimum health. Research demonstrates that the full spectrum of daylight is needed to stimulate our endocrine system properly," says William G. Cooper, president of The Cooper Foundation, Inc., of Lehigh Valley, Pennsylvania, a nonprofit educational organization that offers natural methods of healing to the public. In conjunction with the foundation's work, Cooper produces and hosts two television series, *To Your Health* and *The Young Cry Help*.

Writing in the January-February 1989 issue of the bimonthly newsletter of the Metabolic Research Foundation, of San Ysidro, California, Cooper continues, "Color, in the form of light, is part of the electromagnetic spectrum. In effect, color is a form of energy. As energy-nutrition, as it were—it is reasonable to assume that each color has a different nutritive effect. Generally, foods of a certain color tend to have the same vitamins. Red foods, such as meats and beets, frequently are high sources of B vitamins; yellow-green foods, such as lemons and most greens, are rich in vitamin C.

"Understanding color's connection with food offers a key to maintaining physical health. Everyone is sensitive to the color of food. Appetite will be quickened or dulled, in part, because of the food's color," concludes Cooper.

The Power of Color is about the application of the various colors to beneficially affect the health of the body, mind, emotions, caloric intake for weight control, and pocketbook. Note: *Every color sends out either a high or low vibratory rate that causes in the perceiver a sense of security (warmth) or uncertainty (coolness).* This statement is just one of the little-known facts provided in these pages. My aim as the author is to advise you of the various ways color influences human life. I also want to explain how you can use this knowledge to help yourself and your loved ones. To do this, the book is divided into seven chapters, each of which deals with a major aspect of color.

Chapter One gives the meanings of the individual rainbow colors and explains what exposure to each color can do. Each color has a positive and a negative effect.

Chapter Two explains color as it is understood by physical scientists, who use prisms to evaluate the spectrum. It will also explain color harmony as recognized by artists and stage-lighting technicians.

Chapter Three discusses color in relation to personality and behavior. Personal reactions to particular colors are discussed, as are the psychophysiological effects of color and light in the environment. The meanings of personal color preferences are also interpreted. For example, did you know that people who prefer purple have a good mind, a ready wit, and an ability to make observations that go unnoticed by others?

Chapter Four discusses color and marketing. Marketers use color schemes to sell more products at higher prices. Research has shown that much of a consumer's acceptance of a product depends on the initial impression given by its color. In a controlled blind test similar to the one conducted by Carlton Wagner, consumers complained that the same coffee from different-colored cans was marked by a difference in taste. They said the coffee from a yellow can tasted too weak while the same coffee from a dark brown can was too strong; the coffee from a red can was "rich," and from a blue can, "mild." This chapter also explains how color schemes are used by General Motors, IBM, Sharper Image, Porsche, Holsum Bread, and several airlines.

Practical information on healing with spectral colors is presented in Chapter Five. I cite clinical studies, published in medical journals, that support the more theoretical concepts of color healing, with their modern techniques of application. In addition, I extensively quote several modern color therapy experts, whom I personally interviewed. In this chapter, I also discuss the nine basic postulates for color therapy, which colors are employed by healers from the East and why, the seventeen principles of advanced color healing, color-breathing for self-healing, and the treatment trigger points for helping specific organs and body parts with color therapy.

In Chapter Six, I discuss gemstones, crystals, and birthstones and the many colors that vibrate from their inner cores. I explain how to administer gem chromotherapy on oneself and others. I describe the stones and tell which ones are used for which illnesses. For example, amber is a glowing, tawny stone whose color is reminiscent of the Sun; it is used to treat conditions affecting the throat, such as catarrh, soreness, hay fever, asthma, goiter, and respiratory problems.

Explained in Chapter Seven is color as part of the soul structure. The body and soul give off aural colors that have been recorded by Kirlian photography. In this final chapter, I talk about these aural radiations, which anyone can see using cobalt-blue glasses and which healers claim they can see without any visual aids. I also discuss color vibrations in music and their effects on the body and soul. The study of color is not complete until color is compared to the vibratory frequencies of sound and music.

Men and women are physical beings, but they can be metaphysical by making the body and mind servants of the spirit. Spirit and human interaction are best understood through color and its spiritual and mental counterparts. Colors always produce the same reactions in the human body. Therefore, it is the direct application of aesthetically-pleasing colors through the body that affords complete harmony, with bodily assimilation, revitalization, endurance, and stamina.

People need to replace color energies in their body as they are dissipated and used. Would you like to know how to accomplish such a beneficial replacement? Well, read on! You will learn from these pages about the power of color in replacing lost energy. All of the information in this book will help you use the power of color to your best advantage. Enjoy the knowledge and use it for your benefit as desired!

Morton Walker, D.P.M.
Stamford, Connecticut

Introduction

Throughout history, color has had an effect on mankind. From time immemorial, colors have been symbols of abstract ideas. For instance, green, as in the "green pastures" of the Twenty-Third Psalm, suggests hope or good fortune. Red indicates passion or danger. White in the West is a symbol of innocence and purity. In the Far East, white is symbolic of sadness and mourning, exactly as its opposite—black—is in the West. Yellow can stand for cowardice or treachery, except in its golden, sunny shades wherein it denotes regal power and glory.

However, the abstract ideas associated with any specific color are not universal in significance. The meaning of a color varies according to a person's race, creed, nationality, and even physical, mental, and cultural climate. For example, the ancient Greeks believed that the color of herbal drinks helped to cure diseases. The Hellenic tribes imagined the planet Earth to be composed of four elements—earth, air, fire, and water—and designated earth as green, air as yellow, fire as red, and water as blue.

In early and medieval Christian art, every color had a mystic or symbolic meaning that the church gradually sanctioned. This has been carried over to the modern concepts of the seasons. For example, the colors for Christmas are red and green; for Easter, light blue and pink; for Saint Valentine's Day, red and pale blue; for Saint Patrick's Day, emerald green; and so forth.

In feudal times, heraldic officials used nine symbolic colors to emblazon armorial bearings. Yellow or gold meant honor and loyalty; white or silver, faith and purity; red, courage; blue, piety and resolution; black, grief; green, youth and vitality; purple, high rank; orange, strength and endurance; and violet or amethyst, passion and suffering.

Color affects the totality of our being—the whole quality of our life each day. During our daily existence, colors can hold high distinction, noble grandeur, vital force, meaningful expression, and great consequence. They can cause us to experience visible signs of physical sickness, odd symptoms of mental illness, general indications of emotional instability, a possible uplift of spiritual inspiration, a conditioned response to familiar surroundings, a slow boost into physiological well-being, and various other reactions based on their eight significant factors.

The director of the Wagner Institute for Color Research in Santa Barbara, California, Carlton Wagner, says that the response to color is:

1. *Inherited*. Your endocrine system reacts a certain way to a color because of the neurotransmitters you inherited from your parents. Here is how color plays a role in your hormonal secretions: You see a color, it registers in your brain, and your brain sends out a chemical messenger (a neurotransmitter) for a certain hormonal response from the appropriate endocrine gland. An endocrine gland (a ductless gland) manufactures one or more hormones and secretes them directly into the bloodstream. The endocrine glands include the pituitary, thyroid, parathyroid, and adrenal glands; the ovary and testis; the placenta; and part of the pancreas.

    Endocrine glands react to colors as acknowledged by your brain. For instance, red is exciting to the human brain; therefore, neurotransmitters stimulate the adrenal glands to pump adrenaline into the body.

2. *Learned*. People and events from your past can cause you to like and dislike certain colors in the present. For example, a favorite grade school teacher's blue dress can stimulate an appreciation for blue in your adulthood. Yet, an intense

dislike for that teacher might cause you to "turn off" to blue. In adulthood, you tend to respond to stimuli the way you were conditioned in childhood.

3. *Geographic*. The native colors of a geographic area you like can become your preferred colors. For instance, green could be your favorite color if a rain forest with its lush foliage is a place that helps you feel at ease mentally, spiritually, and physically.

4. *Regional*. Cultural attitudes toward specific colors can vary in different regions.

5. *Light*. The quality and properties of light can cause you to experience the same color differently when the light source changes. Stand at the rim of the Grand Canyon at five o'clock on a summer morning and compare the play of light at that time with the light fourteen hours later when the shadows have grown long and the sunlight has weakened. The color sensations will be different for you.

6. *Climate*. Each season of the year has its own characteristic temperature range and ratio of daylight to darkness. Any Alaskan can tell you about the seasonal depression that tends to come with winter and its daily shortness of light and color.

7. *Income*. All economic groups use status indicators, and color seems to be one of the most important. How you combine colors subtly reflects the class of people you associate with.

8. *Sophistication*. As you grow from your life's experiences, you tend to choose new color preferences.

WHAT COLOR DO YOU FEEL?

Sometimes people describe themselves in colorful terms. They tell others how they feel by saying, "I'm feeling blue," or "I'm seeing red," or "I'm turning green with envy." Sometimes people will say that another person is "acting yellow" (as a coward), or "growing purple with rage," or "falling into the blackness of depression," or "rising in white hope."

Using color to affect or evaluate your own or another person's level of metabolic functioning is called color therapy, known by health professionals as *chromotherapy*. In brief, chromotherapy is the application of color for purposes of healing.

The Pittsburgh Paint Company recently did some experiments with chromotherapy. This paint manufacturer hired painters to work overnight and coat the walls of certain clerical offices in red. Then over the next few days, psychologists observed the office clerks. They soon found that the employees in the red-painted rooms did twice as much work as normal during the first few hours of the workday. Between the third and fourth hours, however, the workers began to show signs of acute agitation. They found fault with their individual office tasks and began arguing with one another.

As the day progressed, coworkers who were long-time friends began fighting with each other verbally and, in some instances, physically. By day's end, even the observing psychologists found themselves irritated and fatigued. The next morning, the workers reported they had felt devastatingly tired the night before and had fallen into bed immediately after their evening meals. Subsequent clinical and laboratory examinations of the participants that were periodically conducted by physicians revealed—among other unusual findings—an exhaustion of the clerks' adrenal glands. The involved psychologists and physicians jointly concluded that people do not work well during a prolonged period in a red-colored room. They are subject to continual stress and suffer from a color syndrome of psychological and physical symptoms. Why? Because the color red is too stimulating.

In contrast, yellow, green, and blue are therapeutic colors. Yellow activates joy. Green, the natural color of plant blood, brings healing. Blue is sedative and pain-relieving.

One evening in 1977, a famous west coast chiropractor and naturopath (who asked not to be identified because of persecution of color therapists in California) was telephoned by the Reverend Everett Strang of Anaheim, California. The Reverend requested this color therapist to attend to Mrs. Strang. Suffering from cancer of the colon, the middle-aged woman was experiencing tremendous pain. Reverend Strang explained that his wife refused to take any pain-relieving drugs. "Is there anything you can do to give her some comfort?" he asked the chiropractor.

The first things the therapist noticed upon entering the patient's room were the red drapes on the windows, a red canopy over the bed, and a red bedspread covering the patient. He suggested, "Let's change the colors in this room right away." He then painted the room's incandescent light bulbs blue.

In about half an hour, the pain had all but subsided for Mrs. Strang. While red is harsh and exciting, blue is palliative and calming. Indeed, blue seems to be a vibratory mitigator of pain.

Colors send out either high or low vibrations that cause the perceiver to sense either coolness or warmth. Red, the longest wavelength, has the slowest vibrational rate; it feels hot to warm. Violet, the shortest wavelength, has the fastest vibrational rate. Colors in the violet-to-blue vibrational range feel cool.

Blind people who have trained their sensory apparatuses are known to "see" colors by holding their hands over them. Sometimes, a blind person's tongue, earlobe, or tip of the nose is more sensitive to color than his fingers.

Colors can be characterized with words that describe how they "feel." They can "sting," "bite," "hit," "press," "pinch," or "blow" on the hand. For strictly descriptive purposes, one could say that red burns, orange warms, yellow feels tepid, green is neutral, and violet cools while pinching.

Orange is an energizing color. Orange and yellow create a laxative effect; they tend to stimulate the elimination of body wastes to such an extent that even the kidneys are cleansed. Thus, orange surroundings encourage defecation and urination. You might try orange with your next bout of constipation. Citrus fruit is the most highly active vibratory food known. Ingesting citrus stirs up more acids in your body than any other food when taken as a juice. However, if you have weak kidneys, you should avoid citrus juice because of how it stimulates micturition.

THE WHOLISTIC PRACTICE OF CHROMOTHERAPY

Chromotherapy—the use of color in the treatment of disease, acceptance of healing, and maintenance of a high level of wellness—can affect illness, body repair, growth, development, and

˒ of life. It's not generally known that color projects a
⎿nd frequency. Yes, the sounds of color—their vibra-
‿⌣⌐⌐—affect your health either positively or negatively. (The
sounds of color will be discussed in detail in Chapter One.) The
remedial use of these color vibrations by therapists is from a
perspective of wholism.

The wholistic practice of chromotherapy deals with the dynamics of healing independent from the treatment of disease.
For this reason, allopathic medical practice (the narrow, traditional viewpoint of exclusively employing drugs for disease) in
its powerful position in the United States has been responsible
for the persecution and prosecution of chromotherapists. In the
past, chromotherapists have been imprisoned for practicing—or
for even just implying that there is such a practice as—color
therapy or healing with color.

For purposes of health enhancement, wholistic practice
adapts the techniques and methods of complementary medicines; chromotherapy is one of the more important complements. Any individual who applies color therapy to himself or
to someone else—even a traditional allopathic physician ori-
ented to drugs and their chemotherapy—is going beyond the
standard medical model. The orthodox medical model is the
science of human pathology geared to medically valid principles for diagnosing and treating illness, injury, and disease.

Chromotherapy takes a tack opposite to that of the medical
model. Applying color healing helps to alleviate the more in-
tangible pathogens. It tends to counter stress, weakness, and
imbalance by fortifying the whole human organism to sustain
homeostasis. Homeostasis is the stability of all body functions
at normal levels.

Chromotherapy increases the ability of the body systems,
functioning together as one whole person, to deal with crises
and to interact with the environment. For example, at Massachusetts General Hospital in Boston, Thomas Fitzpatrick, M.D.,
uses color in the environment as part of his treatment of psoriasis patients with the orally-administered drug methoxsalen.
Thus Doctor Fitzpatrick, an allopathic clinician practicing in an
ultra-orthodox institution, uses color therapy for environmental
interaction. So far, he has escaped prosecution, most likely be-

cause he functions under practice rules closely supervised by the hospital authorities.

At the University Dermatology Clinic in Vienna, Austria, Professor Klaus Wolff, M.D., administers the same treatment as Doctor Fitzpatrick. Using an instrument that resembles a telephone booth, both physicians offer their patients the short wavelength of ultraviolet or black light to activate the methoxsalen. A victim's afflicted skin system—area of psoriasis—responds by reducing lesions and redness, and eliminating scales and itching.

For human psyches, the vibratory beauty of color can inspire, lift, and delight. Everyone needs beauty to cope with the ugliness, misery, and sickness that is part of today's world. It's possible that one tiny wildflower does as much to lift the human spirit as does any dosage of drug. Because beauty is necessary in daily life, we bring flowers to the sick, dress well for visitors, and use cosmetics to enhance our appearance. The beauty that color gives us makes us feel good. We therefore use the beauty from color, allowing it to flow through us, seeing it in our surroundings, creating it in our homes, finding it in our gardens, discovering the ever-present beauty in nature.

I have written this book on the power of color because of my belief that the art and science of color are coming into their own. As you follow the spectrum of color therapeutics and psychology within these pages, you will learn how color's vibratory forces can influence human behavior, metabolic processes, many aspects of health, all manner of activity—nearly everything under the sun. Correction or prevention of illness and imbalance will be found at least in part in the remedial effects of color. Color can make you act "true blue" and keep you feeling "in the pink." By living a colorful life, may you also have stable emotions, a sense of humor, an active mind, a healthy body, glowing enthusiasm, and feelings of fulfillment.

1.

What Is Color?

At any time during the night, put on the light and take a look at the colors that surround you in your bedroom. Then, make sure all the shades are drawn and switch off the lights so that it's as dark as possible. What do you see? Nothing! The colors no longer seem to be in the room. Where did they go? Evidently light is connected with color—but how? Color makes its presence known by waves from the electromagnetic spectrum and the transfer of vibrational energy, both affecting the human brain through your eye's retina.

The *McGraw-Hill Dictionary of Scientific and Technical Terms* defines "color" as a "general term that refers to the wavelength composition of light, with particular reference to its visual appearance." *The Doubleday Dictionary for Home, School, and Office* says it is "a visual attribute of bodies or substances distinct from their spatial characteristics and depending upon the spectral composition of the light emitted or reflected by them."

A favorite theoretical question is, "If a tree falls in the forest and nobody is there to hear it, is there any sound?" Another question might then be, "If colorful art objects are displayed in an exhibit but night has fallen and the room is totally dark, do the objects contain any color?"

The average person recognizes color only in the physical sense. As the second dictionary quote suggests, people see color as that aspect of an object that depends upon the spectral composition of light reaching the eye's retina. Thus, light is

mandatory for the existence of color to the human eye and
mind, declared the Englishman Sir Isaac Newton in 1666. Yet
even in darkness, blind people "see" or feel colors. So, even the
great scientist Newton, the discoverer of gravity, did not realize
there are also other characteristics that define the power of
color.

Writing in *The Therapeutics of Radiant Light and Heat and Convective Heat*, William Benham Snow, M.D., explains how blind
people sense an object's color. According to Doctor Snow:

> Radiant light and heat and color are capable of setting
> up responsive vibrations in animal tissue, inducing re-
> sponses relative to their intensity.
>
> It is readily appreciated that those various frequen-
> cies of color vibrations, affecting, as they do, human tis-
> sue, induce effects relative to their wave lengths and fre-
> quencies. Under varying conditions it will be readily
> appreciated that the judicious employment of the wide
> range of vibratory radiant energy will be in a large mea-
> sure capable either of restoring or inhibiting the vibra-
> tory energies or activities of the animal or human orga-
> nism.

Color, in the form of light, is part of the electromagnetic
spectrum. The other parts of this octave are cosmic rays,
gamma rays, X-rays, ultraviolet rays, infrared rays, radio rays,
and television rays (including light rays), all possessing electromagnetic energy.

WHAT DOES "COLOR" MEAN?

One characteristic of the visual perception of human beings is
generally what's referred to as "color." But what people visualize as color is not all there is to color. In chemistry, color is dye
and pigments. In physics, it is spectral composition. In psychophysics, it is the study of physical stimuli and especially the
perception of physical magnitudes. Two experts on color in the
higher realms, Doctor Bernard Jensen and Doctor Christopher
Hills, place a much greater value on color than does the average
psychologist, chemist, physicist, or other type of scientist. Doc-

tors Jensen and Hills go beyond the physical and mental to also deal with the spiritual conceptions of color.

Still, for educational purposes, I will treat color here strictly in the physical, mental, psychological, and artistic senses as recognized by the average person.

The Impressionist artists, particularly Vincent Van Gogh, could teach us much about observing color. They had a habit of describing everything they saw in the minutest details, including tones and shades. Van Gogh's letters are full of descriptions. For example, in a letter to John Russell, an Australian painter, Van Gogh wrote of a picture by Monet, ". . . a landscape with red sunset and a group of dark fir trees by the sea side. The red sun casts an orange or blood-red reflection on the blue trees and the ground. I wish I could see them."

COLOR AND LIGHT

Color can be described as light of certain wavelengths. Red light has the longest wavelength among the visible colors, and violet light has the shortest. All the other colors are between these two, merging into each other.

As already mentioned, scientist Sir Isaac Newton in 1622 classified light that shines through a prism as having seven distinct colors. He called this group of colors the "spectrum." He said the colors are red, orange, yellow, green, blue, indigo, and violet. Newton's basic and unique color classification—which is different from that of Leonardo Da Vinci, who spoke in the fifteenth century of only four primary colors (red, blue, green, and yellow)—stands today. You can see it in any rainbow, the polar lights, the aurora borealis, and the aurora australis.

All light is visible radiant energy that travels through space in wave forms at a speed of 186,000 miles per second. The light vibrates at different wavelengths, some short, such as ultraviolet, and some long, such as infrared. Modern scientists measure wavelengths of light in angstrom units (AU); each color exhibits a specific AU range. Table 1.1 gives the angstrom unit range from shortest to longest of different colors in the spectrum.

Table 1.1. Wavelengths of the
                Spectral Colors

Color	Angstrom Unit Range
Violet	4300–4600 AU
Blue	4700–5000 AU
Green	5000–5500 AU
Yellow	5800–5900 AU
Orange	5900–6000 AU
Red	6000–6700 AU

The Primary Colors

Red, green, and blue are the primary colors of spectral light because the greatest number of color combinations can be made from them. Red and green lights, for example, make yellow light; red, green, and blue lights combined in equal amounts produce white light.

In paint, the primary colors are red, yellow, and blue. These produce the greatest number of paint colors. If you mix red, yellow, and blue paints, you get black paint.

Colors can be produced by scattering white light. When white light passes through a medium such as air, it is scattered in all directions by the air particles. The short, blue waves are scattered more strongly than the longer yellow waves. This is why the sky appears blue. You can show this very easily by taking a flashlight into a dark room along with a glass of water to which a few drops of plain milk have been added. Shine the light through the water, and look at the flashlight through the glass. The light will appear yellow for the blue waves will be scattered aside. If you look at the glass from the side, it will appear blue.

The Color Spectrum

A beam of light when shining through a glass prism is broken into its constituent wavelengths, represented by bands of color—the spectrum. This *color spectrum* of red, orange, yellow,

The Aurora Borealis

The aurora borealis or northern lights is a faint illumination of the night sky, occurring in the form of rays, bands, and colors, and it is seen on a frequent basis only in the northern latitudes. It is also occasionally seen around Lake Superior in North America and sometimes, though rarely, near the other Great Lakes.

Because the illumination is so faint, the aurora often appears greenish-white in color. When brighter, it shows yellow-green, red, orange-red, or violet-gray, but rarely blue. As seen from central Illinois (as in 1987), the auroral display usually begins with a glow, a faint luminosity that resembles dawn. It is bright near the horizon and gradually fades out above it.

The aurora color display changes, however, and the colorful alterations are magnificent to behold. As it illuminates the sky, it assumes a greenish color (occasionally it is red). This glow is the upper part of an arc that gradually rises above the northern horizon. The arc, which can appear to be in the glow, is seen as part of a great arch across the north, with its highest point near magnetic north. The upper edge fades into the glow. The arc can suddenly have rays resembling searchlight beams. They appear upward from the arc (rayed arc) and the homogeneous character of the arc fades out. The rays are longer than the thickness of the arc and all aim at one point about twenty degrees south of the zenith.

The homogeneous arc can be S-shaped, zigzagged, serpentine, or drapery-like. The drapery is the brightest auroral form and creates a corona or aura (the reason for its name). A flame of light waves shoots upward from the bottom and other patches of luminosity appear. Physicists and astronomers tell us that the number of times the aurora ap-

*pears in a year depends on the number of sunspots and
other significant events on the Sun.*

*The aurora australis of the Southern Hemisphere has
been studied by workers at the Carter Observatory in New
Zealand. It seems to be the exact counterpart of the aurora
borealis, having the same forms and similar distribution.
The two aurora also occur simultaneously.*

green, blue, indigo (violet-blue), and violet has the appearance
of the rainbow.

When physicist Isaac Newton was studying this color spectral phenomenon, he developed the *color wheel*, composed of the twelve rainbow colors from which all the identifiable hues are derived. The color wheel is formed when light is split into its components in a circular shape as it shines through a prism. The color wheel is based on the three *primary colors* of red, yellow, and blue, which are pure colors and cannot be produced by mixing any others. In fact, all 10 million or so of the colors we can perceive begin with just these three. Since every other color under the sun can be made by combining this trio in varying proportions, these three colors are logically known as the primary colors.

Newton laid out his color wheel by spacing the three primaries equidistant around its perimeter. Between each pair of primary colors, he put the color that results from mixing equal parts of the two primaries of the pair: red plus yellow equals orange, yellow plus blue equals green, and blue plus red equals violet.

So, spaced evenly between the primaries are the *secondary colors*: orange, green, and violet. And when a secondary color is mixed with one of the primary colors next to it on the color wheel, a third color is created.

The third set of colors is known as the *tertiary colors*. These colors are made up of equal parts of primaries and secondaries. For example, lime green, which is composed of yellow (a primary) and green (a secondary), is a tertiary color. The tertiaries are the third generation of colors: red-orange, yellow-orange, yellow-green, blue-green, blue-violet (indigo), and red-violet.

The tertiary colors can be mixed with black or white to get the fourth generation or *quaternary color* level. Mixing color after color would eventually produce the 10 million color variations that a human is able to see. And all these colors are variations of just those first three basics—red, yellow, and blue—mixed either with each other or with black or white.

The colors of the spectrum are not ordinarily seen in daily life. Even the colors of the rainbow correspond to a somewhat impure spectrum and have saturations that are considerably lower than those of the pure spectrum. The usual color stimuli are of mixed wavelengths. They are combinations of radiant energy from various parts of the spectrum.

The spectral composition of a color stimulus depends on its mode of production. The light from a soap bubble or from a film of oil on water or from the wing of a butterfly can differ markedly in spectral composition from that of the incident light caused by the interference of light waves. The light from the clear sky or from an opal or from a thin layer of skim milk is richer in short-wave (blue) energy than is incident light. This is because small particles scatter short-wave light more strongly than they scatter long-wave light. This phenomenon of selective scattering accounts not only for the blue coloring of the sky, opals, skim milk, and blue eyes, but also for the orange and red coloring of the setting sun and the apparent fire of the opal because the transmitted energy is deprived of short-wave components through the scattering.

COLOR TERMS

The subject area of color brings with it, as can be expected, its own terminology. Many of the terms are common words used every day by most people.

A *tint* is a tone of color produced by adding white to a color. Tinting can produce an effect that is often only marginally different from the principal color. The handy umbrella word that covers all tints is *pastel*. A pastel appears soft and gentle, produced by adding a great amount of white to a color. Some ex-

The Artistry of Mixing Paints

Mixing paints to attain color shades is similar to, and yet somewhat different from, mixing stage lights. It's true that both the painter at his easel and the lighting technician backstage achieve certain colors by mixing other colors. But the important difference between the two processes can be illustrated by mixing amber light with blue light on-stage and amber paint with blue paint on a pallet. The electrician will get white light. The artist will get green paint.

Usually, it is difficult to predict the exact color that will be produced by mixing pigments. A careful study would have to be made of the different colors that the paints reflect. It is usually easier to test the colors by actual experiment. To obtain a desired color, many different pigments are often mixed until the proper color is achieved. Then the artist's formula for making the color can be recorded. Red, yellow, and blue are the basic colors in pigment, whereas red, green, and violet are the basic colors in light.

amples of pastels are pink, made from red; lilac, made from purple; and apricot, made from orange. Pastels are close to white and rank very high on the value scale.

The *value* of a color is the degree or concentration of lightness or darkness of the color relative to all other colors. For example, yellow has a higher value than green, and green has a higher value than purple.

Hue is the distinguishing attribute of a chromatic color that makes it red, green, blue, etc. A hue or particular shade or tint of a color can vary in *intensity*, which refers to the depth of a color. For example, emerald green can be a pale emerald or a deep, intense emerald. Both are officially emerald green, but they differ in their intensity.

Shades are the tones closer to black on the value scale. Lilac is a pastel; royal purple is the opposite, deeply shaded with black.

Texture or *finish* is another important characteristic that affects how dark or light a color appears. A color with a lustrous, shiny finish will look lighter than the same color with a dull or matte finish. This is why a silk pillow looks brighter and lighter than the velvet couch it was meant to match.

Technical Color Terms

Scientists and craftsmen who study the application of color for creative purposes have their own technical vocabulary.

An object that contains color is considered *chromatic*. An object that has no color is *achromatic*. Colors are seen by an artist or photographer as either chromatic (possessing a hue) or achromatic (without a hue). In contrast to the simple definition of hue offered earlier, a more technical definition is: Hue is that attribute of chromatic color that determines if a color is red, yellow, green, blue, or an intermediate in the color spectrum. Red, yellow, green, and blue are called the "psychologically primary hues" because nearly all people use them to describe the chromatic colors they experience.

Saturation is the attribute that determines a color's degree of difference from the achromatic color that looks most nearly like it. All the achromatic colors—white, gray, black, silver, and crystal clear—have zero saturation.

The color of an object has the attributes of hue, saturation, and *lightness*. The lightness of the color of an object is the degree to which the object reflects or transmits light. The achromatic colors of opaque objects vary in lightness only from black to white. However, the colors of objects that transmit light without any scattering vary in lightness all the way from black to perfectly clear.

On the other hand, the color of a light has the attributes of hue, saturation, and *brightness*. Brightness is the degree to which a self-luminous area emits light. Brightness varies from invisible to dazzling.

Using an instrument made with different colors of glass, you can analyze color by breaking up its reflecting white light into a spectrum. Do you know why and how we sense color, witness color analysis, see color happen, or recognize the color spectra that form?

Color can be defined as that element of visual perception that lets you distinguish the differences between two optical fields that are otherwise identical. As you observe, you see color variations between the two fields as the result of the spectral synthesis of the two light beams that illuminate them. Thus, the sense of color is closely intertwined with the sense of vision. Both senses—color and vision—are subjective concepts, however, which are examined in more detail in the next section.

HOW WE SENSE COLOR

People experience color from memory, in dreams, and from pressure on or electrical stimulation of the eyeball or optic nerve. But the usual stimulus for color is a change in the spectral composition of the radiant energy that is incident (immediately present) to the central part of the retina in the eye. Radiant energy is the energy traveling through space in the form of electromagnetic waves and is defined by its distribution according to wavelength. The effects that radiant energy has on matter also depend greatly on wavelength.

Some of the longer waves are called radio waves; some are called Hertzian waves (after Heinrich Rudolph Hertz, the German physicist) and are used in radar and television; some are called X-rays or Roentgen rays (the latter after Wilhelm Konrad Roentgen, another German scientist); and some are gamma rays, which are high-energy photons.

Only the radiant energy whose wavelength falls into one particular octave (between 380 and 760 millimicrons) of the whole electromagnetic spectrum can be detected by the human eye. Therefore, the usual stimulus for color comes only from this small part of the total electromagnetic spectrum.

If the radiant energy coming from a heated body, such as the filament of an incandescent lamp, is passed through a prism, the visible part of the resulting spectrum has colors whose hues range continuously from red, at the long-wave end, through orange, yellow, green, and blue to violet, at the short-wave end. For a daylight-adapted individual with normal color vision, the stimuli for colors of the psychologically primary hues closely approximate the following: blue, 480 millimicrons (mmc); green, 515 mmc; yellow, 575 mmc; and red, 650 mmc.

The brightness of the colors of a prismatic spectrum produced with an incandescent lamp will vary from invisible at each extreme (at about 380 and 760 mmc) to a maximum brightness at around 580 mmc. The saturation of these colors will also vary greatly, going from zero at each extreme of the spectrum to a high maximum at around 650 mmc.

Selective Absorption by Pigments and Dyes

The greatest impact on the human eye by a color stimulus comes by far from the phenomenon of selective absorption, a characteristic of pigments and dyes whereby the energy absorbed varies with the wavelength. Selective absorption of vegetable pigments is revealed in nature by the green of live foliage, the brown of dead foliage, and the many colors of flowers. Selective absorption of light by animal pigments enables human beings to see the brown of human skin, the red of blood, and the yellow, red, brown, and black of hair. Finally, the selective absorption of light by natural and synthesized dyes and pigments gives human beings control over the colors of painted surfaces, textiles, plastics, ceramics, printed papers, and other objects of the civilized world.

Pigments are used to color paints, plastics, paper, and ceramics. Since pigment particles are by definition not soluble in the medium in which they are dispersed, the pigmented medium, in addition to absorbing and transmitting the incident radiant energy, also scatters some of it. This light-scattering property of pigmented media is desirable because it gives a film of paint the ability to hide the surface to which it is applied. It also gives opacity to layers of paper, plastic, and ceramic.

The color stimulus produced by a pigmented film can be evaluated with a spectrophotometer, which has a prism or diffraction grating for dispersing incident light into its component spectral parts and a photometer for comparing the reflected light with the incident light for each of the spectral parts.

Some energy is reflected better in one part of the visible spectrum than in another. A film of vivid red paint reflects the long-wave part of the spectrum as strongly as a film of white paint. However, red's reflectance in other parts of the spectrum, though low, is by no means zero. Some energy is reflected throughout all of the visible spectrum.

COLOR HARMONY

When two or more colors are used near each other and produce a pleasing effect, they are said to be in *color harmony*. Selecting colors to be used together is part of the job for the artist, architect, interior decorator, industrial designer, landscape gardener, dressmaker, stage designer, and other creators and buyers of merchandise. It can be tricky since several factors may need to be considered.

Harmonious colors are colors close to each other in warmth or coldness. For example, a harmonious monochromatic color scheme could include a light tone such as pearl gray, a medium tone such as flannel gray, and a deep tone such as charcoal.

Related colors are either *monochromatic*—the same color but in a variety of shades—or *analogous*—near each other on the color wheel. Either way, the colors are related and, as in any good family situation, the relatives get along well.

Contrasting colors, as the name implies, are complementary colors. Sir Isaac's handy color wheel shows they are directly opposite each other. In technical terms, a contrast is made by putting a secondary color against a primary; in common usage, however, the term has a much broader meaning and can refer, for example, to black set against white or brown set against cream. A small quantity of a contrasting color is often useful as an accent in a room or clothing.

Contrasting colors as used in decorating are colors that are as *un*alike as possible. Red and green, yellow and violet, and orange and blue are all complements or contrasting colors. That's why red and green used together make Christmas such a visually stimulating season, while yellow and violet vibrate in spring bouquets and autumn's orange leaves stand out against a blue sky. Indoors, however, contrasting color schemes must be used with some finesse.

To get one primary's *complementary color*, the other two primaries are mixed together. Therefore, the complementary color of red is green (a mixture of blue and yellow), the complementary color of blue is orange (red and yellow), and the complementary color of yellow is violet (red and blue). When equal quantities of two complementary colors are mixed together, they form gray. In design terms, however, the definition of complementary is less strict and generally just refers to colors that go well together.

Color harmony also involves personal likes and dislikes. Many people get tired of old color combinations and often welcome any change whatsoever. Sometimes people get used to a color combination they disliked and even begin to like it. In addition, color harmony cannot be separated from design. The shape and relative size of the areas of color to be combined often govern their choice. Here, chromatic adaptation comes into play. A large red area can make a central grayish-red spot look green after a while. This instability is usually unpleasant. However, a vivid red spot on a grayish-red background is stable and pleasant. The rule prescribing the use of highly saturated colors only as accents in small areas can be traced back to chromatic adaptation.

Color harmony also depends on the absolute angular size of the areas covered with color. A beautifully designed mosaic pattern magnified by a factor of ten might produce a garish and unpleasant effect. The individual colors will thus be seen to have high saturations and to differ greatly. What was seen as a subdued and even subtle color effect in miniature becomes an over-emphasized caricature when magnified.

Some colors spontaneously attract our attention and gain our preference while others repel us. This is not by chance, but rather follows specific principals of color harmony. The appropriateness of the color to the object, the color's warmth or coolness, and whether it advances or retreats must all be considered together.

Every rule of color harmony, no matter how simple, is only partly true. There are, however, four respected principles: *order, familiarity, common aspect,* and *avoidance of ambiguity.*

1. *Order.* Color harmony is achieved by selecting and arranging colors according to a coordinated plan.

2. *Familiarity*. Color harmony is achieved by using the sequences that people know. Nature is the true guide to color harmony. One human preference is for straight lines fanning upward from a black point in a color solid, one for each shadow series. Another preference is for a tilted ellipse centered on the neutral axis of a color solid.

3. *Common aspect*. Color harmony is achieved by reducing the clash of two clashing colors. For example, when two paint colors clash, put some of each into the other and mix. This reduces the difference between the two colors. However, it is advisable to use all colors of the same lightness.

4. *Avoidance of ambiguity*. Color harmony is achieved by combining colors with no hue differences that are unpleasant. To do this, Albert Henry Munsell, the American portrait painter, developed the Munsell scale. The Munsell scale shows a sampling of all colors ranked for hue, value, and chroma on a 100-point scale. It has ten hues with twenty hue steps for each of the main divisions: red, yellow-red, yellow, green-yellow, green, blue-green, blue, purple-blue, purple, and red-purple. When a person with normal color vision views the specimens in the *Munsell Book of Color*, he sees that specimens having the same Munsell hue notation actually do have nearly the same hue. The Munsell color notations are for everyday use. Colors whose hues are complementary to a daylight-adapted observer, along with triads that are equally spaced in hue, are stable and have a chance of forming color harmony.

COLOR CHARACTERISTICS AND EFFECTS

Each color has its unique characteristics and own special way of affecting people. The research on colors is ongoing, but the following descriptions are based on the most recent data.

Red

Red is a color that stirs the senses and passions. It is associated with the power, energy, vitality, and excitement of life. In its positive aspect, red can stimulate strength, joy, happiness, and love. It is one of the primary colors of fire, and the deep red of scarlet can stimulate the animal nature, the baser physical passions. The crimson of blood represents the suffering elements in life. The gentle pink shade can evoke the mother-love vibration. Red is personal, the color of greatest warmth. The negative aspect of the red vibration can bring out fear, uncontrolled passion, lust, and excessive anger. Red can be used when vitality is low or blood circulation is poor. It is the color most disturbing to people with mental problems or neuroses, and it should not be used around them. It has the slowest vibration of all the visible colors, affecting the emotions quicker than any other.

Orange

Orange stimulates creativity and ambition along with energetic activity. It can also generate pride and a sense of preservation of self, others, animals, plants, and objects. But excessive exposure to orange can produce great nervousness and restless behavior. Many fruits and vegetables are orange or orange-red, making this a color of nourishment. (Horticulturist Luther Burbank found that orange light speeds up the growth of plants.) Among minerals, orange represents attraction of the elements, working as a cohesive atomic force.

Yellow

Yellow is primarily a joyous color, but it also brings out wisdom, understanding, and the highest of intuitional insight. In its golden aspect, yellow represents spiritual perfection, peace, and rest. It is the color of sunshine, youth, gladness, and merriment. Characteristically, yellow makes sunless rooms bright and cheery when used as a wall color. It is a good color to paint the kitchen. Yellow fruits and vegetables tend to act as a laxative to the bowel and calm the nerves. In its most positive vibration, golden yellow is deeply spiritual, bringing out compassion and creativity. In its negative aspect, however, yellow, when too bright or used too often, is overstimulating to the psyche and nerves and can cause mental irritation even to the point of destructiveness. Yellow in its negative vibration is also the color of cowardice, prejudice, and destructive domination.

Green

Green is nature's color, from the pale green of new spring grass and budding leaves to the deep green of the mature forest. Green is soothing, healing, peaceful, and cool in its positive aspect. It's a restful balm for people who are weary in body or mind. Green has great healing power. On its negative side, green represents selfishness, jealousy, and laziness. Heavy, dark greens can be depressing and even debilitating. Green is useful in soothing pain and calming a teething infant. Yellow-green stimulates generosity on the mental plane and the body's elimination of wastes on the physical plane. Spring green represents new life, regeneration, joy, and gladness.

Blue

Blue is the color of the heavenly consciousness, truth, harmony, calmness, and hope. Sky-blue clothing worn by women can bring out the gentlemanly protective nature in men. Whereas red excites the passions, blue soothes and quiets them. The softer hues of blue can sedate the nerves. Blue is a quieting color and is used in the rooms of violent criminals and mental patients. Soft blue clothing provides the greatest protection against the sun's rays in the tropics. In its negative aspect, too much blue can be depressing, bringing on a feeling of the "blues" in otherwise healthy people. Blue and green together can stimulate the highest level of talent and creativity in art and music.

Indigo

Indigo in the spectrum is lodged between blue and violet. In its highest positive vibration, it combines reason with intuition and discipline with creativity. It simultaneously represents the creative and destructive forces in a person's nature. It also represents the metabolic process in man (catabolism and anabolism) and the divine law of change and growth. In its negative aspect, indigo stands for stagnation, mental fatigue, and striving without success. But it also represents the "breakthrough point" where old failures transmute into new successes, frustrated mental striving breaks through to higher consciousness, and problems turn into stepping stones to wonderful solutions. Indigo represents the healing crisis of the natural healing art, where old toxins and wastes are cast out of the body to make room for new tissue.

Violet

Violet in its highest vibration represents good motives, elevated spiritual aspirations, and enhanced consecration of the soul. The purple robe or mantle has long been a symbol of royalty and spiritual authority. Violet is associated with prosperity, wealth, and increased productivity. Stimulating the spiritual nature of man, the violet vibration offers self-mastery, higher realms of creativity, and royal consciousness. (The nineteenth-century German musical genius Richard Wagner is said to have composed his greatest works in rooms decorated with purple velvet drapes.) The pale violet of orchids is the vibration of the truth seeker. In its negative aspect, violet can overwhelm a person unprepared for the snobbery, pretense, and even deceit it can generate. Violet is the fastest vibration among the rainbow colors, fading quicker than any other.

White

White is the vibration of purity and the cosmic plane of perfection. It represents harmony in the way it blends all the rainbow colors. The power of white light is intolerable to people who cultivate such base characteristics as deceit, malice, jealousy, hate, envy, and violence. White light is the great revealer of ultimate truth.

Black

Black represents the absence of light and, as a pigment or color, it absorbs the least amount of spectral light. Black, the opposite of white, is the color of the funeral drape and represents the loss or absence of life. In the West, a black armband is worn to symbolize grief over the loss of a loved one or somebody greatly respected. Being around black too much can drain a person's health because black absorbs energy and vitality, leaving behind physical and mental fatigue. Black clothing interferes with the proper elimination of toxins through the skin and can bring out a mood of somberness. The less black clothing a person wears in hot weather, the more comfortable that person will feel. In its most negative aspect, black is said to encourage the worst in people with criminal tendencies; the darkest deeds are reputedly done at night, and the worst villain is called "black-hearted."

Brown

Brown in its most positive aspect represents fertility, Mother Earth, and the strength of seasoned wood. However, brown is a heavy, severe color with a slow vibration that also has many negative effects. Brown should be used sparingly in home decoration and clothing, and is best when used with other colors such as white, red, orange, and yellow. In its negative aspect, brown repulses the opposite sex, diminishes personal vitality, negates the life force, and implies decay and the dying of nature. The highest quality of brown is its representation of the plane from which beauty comes forth, as the mud from which the lily or rose grow; but the color reflects no beauty in itself. Because brown, black, and gray (a mixture of white and black) reflect no self-beauty, they can be effectively used as a backdrop for a beautiful object, such as a piece of pottery or sculpture, and can emphasize the beauty of other colors when used as the frame or trim color.

Considering the Colors for Personal Application

Each color has a positive and negative effect on mental attitude. We live in the mind. The power of mind over body and color together is one factor in our mind's eye, even in dreams. The pupil of the eye relaxes more when it looks at a beautiful scene or picture than when it looks at something ugly or horrible. It also

Various Substances Possess Different Wavelengths of Light

If you darken your kitchen, place a pinch of salt or soda on the end of a screwdriver or piece of tin, and hold the salt or soda in a gas flame, what will happen?

Even the tiniest speck of salt will cause a colorless, almost invisible flame to take on a strong yellow glow. The yellow color is due to the vapor of the chemical element sodium, which is one of the components of common salt.

If you passed the light from this flame through a prism, you would find that, unlike sunlight or the light from an electric lamp, this light has only one color from the spectrum—a narrow region in the yellow part of the spectrum and nothing else. Any chemical that contains sodium will give off light of this same color regardless of what it may be mixed or combined with. The waves of yellow light that come from a sodium-fed flame are about twenty-three-millionths of an inch in length.

In the same way, a little cream of tartar or saltpeter introduced into a gas flame gives the flame a peculiar lilac color, and the light given off is found to consist of only two definite wavelengths—one in the red and another in the violet. Compounds of calcium give off an orange-red flame, and compounds of barium give off a vivid green flame. In each case, definite wavelengths of light are emitted.

relaxes more when you feel love than when you feel hate or fear. The subconscious mind can also see and behold colors.

The sensitive colors of light hues are the spiritual ones. With them, you can meditate easier when you need to quiet your inner self. Spiritual colors are for you if you feel deeply, have fair skin and fine hair, or wish to reach out to the ethereal and aesthetic in nature and the soul. By developing the faculty to go alone into silence, you can project a soft hue or gentle tint as an overlay on any scene or picture. You just need to see things from a spiritual standpoint rather than from a physical one.

When dealing with argumentative people, change the color of the anger displayed by your opponent from red to blue and see your opponent in your mind's eye with that gentler tint. This will help you to remain calm. Conversely, perk up a "blue Monday" by looking through a pair of imaginary "rose-colored glasses." You can change much of the bad in your world into good just by using colors, both in reality and in your mind.

2.

The History of Color

Color is the most malleable, the most exciting, the most immediately noticeable, and possibly the most moving component of mankind's history on Earth. It has pushed people into action when they might never have progressed as the guardians of the Earth.

There are four main parts to the study of color history. They are the psychologic history of color, sociologic history of color, scientific history of color, and historic use of color.

THE PSYCHOLOGIC HISTORY OF COLOR

Colors have an emotional appeal, typified by your own reactions to them, even if they are just described in words. Whether you realize it or not, you probably associate every color with some particular feeling, behavior, lesson, action, experience, environment, or event in your personal past. That's how it has been throughout history for mankind. The mindset of individuals, groups, tribes, countries, and cultures evolves from past uses and associations of color.

Color has energy that impacts on you psychologically and, in turn, physiologically. Variations in the number of impacts upon your eyes affect the muscular, mental, and nervous activity of your body. For example, tests by engineers at the Pittsburgh Plate Glass Company, as described in the company's booklet *Color Dynamics for the Home,* indicate that under ordinary light, muscular activity takes twenty-three empirical units. It increases slightly under blue light. Green light increases it a little more, to about twenty-eight units. Yellow light then raises it to thirty units. If you are subjected to a certain color for even as little as five minutes, your mental and muscular activity will change according to your psychological response to that color. In other words, your psychological response to a color can affect you physically.

Instinctively knowing this, leaders throughout history—especially those who led armies into battle—have utilized colors in the form of banners, flags, buntings, uniforms, and trophies. The colors they chose had their soldiers stirred with emotion. American Indian warriors and primitive natives inhabiting the South American and African jungles used the psychology of color in the form of war paint to frighten their enemies and identify their friends.

Long before Hippocrates, the medical profession realized that colors can be used to stimulate and depress. Some shades help people relax and be cheerful. Others stimulate and invigorate them. Still others cause irritation and actual physical discomfort. The Aztecs of ancient Mexico are said to have used irritating colors as devices of torture.

The Pittsburgh Plate Glass Company booklet says that the psychological application of color was originally developed to increase efficiency in industry. Indeed, in scores of large factories, such applications brought about changes in production that are truly phenomenal. Colors as a result became a part of manufacturing processes during the Industrial Revolution.

William J. Faber, D.O., medical director of the Milwaukee Pain Clinic and Metabolic Research Center in Milwaukee, Wisconsin, affirms that the mind and body are affected by color. Doctor Faber says that both an advantageous physiological effect on his clinic's patients and increased production among the clinic employees have occurred from the application of the psychology of color. The clinic's interior is painted a pale blue. New offices that Doctor Faber decorated with the help of color therapists helped him and his staff to become more productive while at the same time more efficient in their movements. Doctor Faber's patients have said in questionnaires and surveys that the office colors help them feel less pain after they have been on the premises for only five minutes.

Starting about 1910, near the time of Henry Ford, testimonials have been taken from industrialists on how certain colors reduce workers' eye fatigue, lift spirits, and improve quality and quantity in all kinds of hard-goods manufacturing. Accidents have been reduced, too. Certain colors used in hospitals have helped speed the recovery of patients and raise the efficacy of action of medical and nursing staffs.

Students and teachers have reported that in school, concentration is assisted, energy is stimulated, and eye fatigue is retarded by particular colors, such as varying shades of green and blue. Leading hotels have utilized color dynamics to impart an atmosphere of friendliness, comfort, and good cheer. Offices can be made to seem more spacious and pleasing to the eyes, contributing to the good health and efficiency of employees.

All aspects of behavior and personality are acted upon by the various colors. For a more detailed discussion of these psychological effects, plus what your favorite color says about you, please see Chapter Three.

THE SOCIOLOGIC HISTORY OF COLOR

The second part to our study of color history concerns the sociology of color. This is the study of man's social interaction with, and interpretation of, the various colors.

Black

Black is said to be the first color recognized by mankind, although black and white are at either end of the neutrals range and are not really colors at all. Black, in fact, is colorless from the absence or complete absorption of light, while white is a blend of all the colors of the rainbow in perfect balance. White mixed with black produces a whole series of grays that links these two implacable opposites. A popular figure of speech says that people who hold strong opinions see things in black and white, while people who are liberal-minded think more in terms of gray.

During the time of the city-states of ancient Greek culture (around 1000–322 B.C.), black symbolized life because the day was born out of the dark. During the sixteenth century, Anne of Brittany used black for mourning, and this association has now existed through several centuries. Black is also symbolic of evil, old age, and silence. It is strong and sophisticated. Its primary use in modern interior decoration is for small quantities of accent because its morbid connotation actually heightens other colors to produce cheerfulness.

Red

According to some anthropologists, red was the second color primitive man was able to distinguish. During the time of the knights of the Round Table, red was associated with blood and therefore life. Later, it was associated with fire and therefore danger. Red is also a symbol of love, vigor, and action. Bright red is such a forceful color that its use, as with black, is usually limited to small areas of accent in clothing and interior design. Light values of red make warm background colors. Red was a major color for certain ancient cultures, such as the Chinese, Japanese, and Asian Indians. It goes back 5,000 years in recorded history.

Yellow

Yellow has had numerous associations throughout history. As a color sacred to the Chinese and important to the Egyptians and Greeks, yellow gradually became a symbol of power. Because of this symbolism, its use was frowned upon by the early Christians who gathered around the apostles of Jesus Christ. China's emperors owned "exclusive rights" to wear yellow. It was the only color that they and members of their royal family could wear. Moreover, Chinese commoners were never allowed to wear it. Yellow has been associated with deceit, cowardice, and jealousy as well as with wisdom, gaiety, and warmth. Yellow, in its many hues, shades, and values, is a choice color in interior decoration to brighten a home (especially the kitchen) and hospital room.

White

White was used in times past in shrouds, or burial robes, and was the color of mourning in ancient Rome and medieval France. White is symbolic of purity, innocence, faith, peace, and surrender. Off-white is applied extensively in home decoration because of the sense of cleanliness it imparts.

Blue

Blue is thought by anthropologists to have been unidentified as a separate color for the first few thousand years of modern man; until around 5000 B.C., it was considered a form of black. The Hebrews, however, did not distinguish between blue and purple. Blue is the rarest color in nature—hence the origin of the terms "true blue" and "blue blood." It is the symbol of happiness, hope, truth, honor, repose, and distance. In its various hues, it is widely used in medical practice, clothing, and interior design.

Green

Green has not always been a popular color, although it is abundant in nature. Because of its use in pagan ceremonies, green was banned by the early Christians. It was later adopted by Robin Hood and his band and stands as a symbol of their life and vigor. It is a sacred color to the Moslems. Green is associated with luck, particularly by the Irish. It is, of course, also a sociological trademark for the Irish. It denotes life, spring, hope, and also envy. It is cool enough to be restful, yet warm enough to be friendly. Green is applied extensively in home decorating, but in clothing, it is seldom worn as a suit or coat.

Purple

Purple is an ancient color. Once costly to produce because the dye was so difficult to keep colorfast, it became a symbol of royalty and was thus avoided by the early Christians. Associated with the spiritual, with mystery, with humility, with penitence, and with wisdom, purple is a dignified color. Mauve, plum, eggplant, and other shades of purple are frequently employed in dignified, elegant rooms.

Brown

Brown was the color assigned to peasants during the Middle Ages (about A.D. 500–1500) and is thus associated with humility. It makes people think of autumn, the harvest, nature, and decay. Brown ranges from yellow to red in cast. Even though it is dark and neutral, it has considerable richness and depth. The wood used in most traditional furniture is brown.

Gray

Gray is a somber color. It was the color worn by the common people during the time of Charlemagne, the king of the Franks in the eighth century and the first emperor of the Holy Roman Empire. It was also worn a great deal by the Quakers. Gray is associated with retirement, sadness, modesty, and indifference. It can have a warm or a cool cast, though it is mainly cool. Situated between the two extremes of white and black, gray seems to be society's most accepted neutral color. It often is a good background color in artistic renditions, clothing ensembles, buildings, machinery coloration, and room design.

Color was first used by primitive man to mark his cave walls to claim his dwelling. The next practical uses of manmade color were for adornment, such as in rituals and as makeup (crude cosmetics); to mark trees and rocks (signs in the forest); and in clothing and furnishings. Colorings as marking materials came from roots, berries, bark, and chemicals.

THE SCIENTIFIC HISTORY OF COLOR

Have you ever noticed the beautiful rainbow that is sometimes produced when a beam of sunlight passes through the water spray from a waterfall or garden sprinkler? That simple observation could be the starting point of a scientist's search for the cause of the many colors. If you are that scientist, you might ask, "Why are the rainbow colors formed?" You would then experiment and study to find the answer.

Some of the earliest attempts to scientifically analyze color were made by curious persons who wanted to find out what caused the rainbow. For example, in the year 1611, Marco Antonio de Dominis, the archbishop of Spalato (Spalato is now part of Yugoslavia), erroneously suggested that the rainbow was produced by light being reflected from within raindrops and passing through different thicknesses of water. In the seventeenth century, Rene Descartes, the French philosopher-mathematician, thought colors were made by light spreading out.

Both Marco Antonio and Descartes were partly wrong, but they were partly correct, too. According to Sir Isaac Newton, who finally found the answer late in the seventeenth century, the colors of the rainbow are made by reflection and refraction, that is, the bending of light by the atmosphere or medium through which it must travel.

While studying the rainbow, scientists involved with optics passed to the more basic puzzle of the colors themselves. They wondered what causes the difference between red and yellow, or blue and green. The most widely accepted viewpoint today is that light sometimes acts as if it is made of waves, shaped somewhat like water waves. The differences between colors are due to the differences in the lengths of their waves. For example, green colors have shorter wavelengths than yellow colors. All the colors fall between the shortest wavelength of violet and the longest one of red. The colors merge into each other, but the lines of light from which they evolve can be analyzed for a better understanding of all the aspects of the spectrum.

Lines of Light in Spectrum Analysis

At about the time of the American Civil War, two scientists at the University of Heidelberg in Germany, Robert Bunsen and Gustav Kirchhoff, performed the first experiments with spectrum analysis. These scientists examined the spectra of a large number of chemicals and found that the wavelengths of the light each chemical gave off varied with the chemical. They determined that color analysis could be used to identify a substance instead of the usual inconvenient and time-consuming methods of chemical analysis. Color analysis now became simpler and faster than ever before.

Bunsen and Kirchhoff's method of spectrum analysis necessitates only the vaporization of the substance being tested in a flame or, better, in an electric arc or spark. If it is a gas, the substance can be put into a vacuum tube and made to glow by passing a high-voltage current through it. Some of the light from the substance can then be passed through a prism, and the exact nature of the spectrum can be noted. Once this has been done with a large number of substances, the spectrum of an unknown mixture can be readily identified.

A spectroscope is used for this analysis. Instead of an eyepiece, it uses a photographic plate or film to make a permanent record called a spectrograph.

Each wavelength of light from the substance being tested is represented on the spectrograph by a sharp line, an image of the slit through which the light was passed. Several lines can fall in each color region of the spectrum. The spectrographic film itself is not in color; the only important factor is the relative positioning of the lines on the film.

Electrons produce these lines of light when their atoms are stimulated by heat or electricity. The electrons in an atom from a certain substance can vibrate in only one way, giving rise to a definite set of wavelengths of light. But this is true only if the substance is a gas and its atoms are independent of each other. In a solid substance, neighboring atoms jostle each other and blur their characteristic waves into a jumble consisting of all possible wavelengths. Therefore, the spectral colors of solid substances cannot be easily analyzed this way.

The Bunsen and Kirchhoff breakthrough advanced mankind by furnishing a means for evaluating not just the spectral colors themselves, but also minerals, chemicals, human tissues, and other organic and inorganic materials. It opened all aspects of the history of the universe to human exploration. Indeed, the discipline of spectral analysis is as significant in the development of human intelligence and knowledge as the invention of the wheel.

Color Analysis With Prisms

A triangular-shaped piece of glass called a prism *breaks up white light passing through it into a rainbow-like pattern called a* spectrum. *Using a prism, you can analyze any shade of color by breaking it into its basic, component colors. To do this, place the prism between a source of white light and a screen. The white light should be shielded so that only a narrow beam of it can pass through a slit and shine on the prism. The colors of the spectrum produced on the screen always will be in the same order: red, orange, yellow, green, blue, indigo, and violet.*

When you place a piece of red glass between the prism and the screen, the only color in the spectrum that shows up brightly on the screen will be red. Some of the other colors may appear—but very faintly. Thus, red glass will be seen as red simply because it permits mainly red light to pass through. Blue glass permits only blue to come through to the screen; almost all the other rays are absorbed. Green glass does the same thing for green. But a color like purple, which is not observed as a basic color in the spectrum, will allow both red and blue light to come through in about equal amounts, and the middle of the spectrum will be gone. From this analysis, you may conclude that purple is a combination of the two fundamental colors red and blue, and you will be correct.

Playing With Colored Lights

This process of passing light through glass is called color subtraction. *It is subtraction because the glass takes away or absorbs different colors from the spectrum. Suppose you*

reverse the process and add light of one color on top of light
of another color. This is exactly what happens when colored
lights are used on a stage—turn on red and blue lights at
the same time and place, and they combine to form a purple
spotlight on stage. Furthermore, you can mix lights of different colors in all sorts of proportions. Add a small amount
of red light to white light and you will get pale red or pink.
Add some green to white and you will get pale green.

Next, if you aim the spectrum formed by the prism on a
red object, you will notice that the places where yellow,
green, blue, indigo, and violet formerly appeared in the
spectrum now appear as dark regions on the red object. But
the part of the object where the red light falls appears as
very bright red. The red object absorbs (subtracts) all the
colors but red. If blue light strikes the red object, it is not
reflected. Instead, it is absorbed and its energy is converted
into heat. Since little or no blue light is reflected, the blue
portion of the spectrum appears dark on the red object. The
same is true for all the other colors that strike the object except red. The green light is absorbed. The violet light is absorbed. Only the red light is reflected.

In the same way, a blue-colored object reflects blue but
absorbs all the other colors. A purple object reflects red and
blue, and absorbs the other colors. Thus, the color of an
opaque object depends on the color it reflects, provided the
object is not a source of light. Actually, few colored objects
reflect just one color. For example, a green leaf reflects
mainly green but also small amounts of other spectrum colors. A red tomato reflects mainly red but also other spectrum colors to a slight extent.

In summary, a red glass is red because it lets through
mainly red light and absorbs the other colors, but purple
glass lets through a mixture of red and blue-violet light
while absorbing the colors in the middle of the spectrum.

All of this is the science and art of spectral analysis.
Spectral analysis is important to industry. When a chemi-

cal element is heated to the gaseous state in a flame or electric arc, it gives off light. If this light is passed through a
special instrument called a spectroscope, it then appears as
a number of separate bright lines and is called a line spectrum. Each element has its own definite bright-line spectrum by which it can be identified. These spectra are used
by scientists to test and analyze materials in industry and
science. The chemical elements in the Sun and other stars
are identified by these spectra, too.

THE HISTORIC USE OF COLOR

Centuries ago, in the land of the Nile River, the Egyptians wor-
shipped the healing power of the Sun. Their god of creation, as
the legend goes, crossed the sky each day in a boat called *Mil-
lions of Years*. This Sun god was considered the giver of health
and prolonger of life. He had different names, depending upon
the time of day and where he was located in the sky. He was
called Khepri in the morning, Re at noon, and Atum in the evening. He performed miracles of healing according to the spectral colors produced at the different hours of the day, and it was
an Egyptian's religious duty to literally take a daily bath in the
spectral light of the Sun.

In another time and place, the Incas of Mexico also wor-
shipped the Sun. Their conquests were partly religious cru-
sades carried on for the purpose of forcing all people to accept
the Sun god as the ruling deity with power over life, death,
health, and disease. The colors of their Sun god were red,
white, blue, and green, but not gray.

Mythology holds the sunlight's spectrum to be a prime
source of longevity, health, and healing. The Sun, therefore, is
a form of mythological hero. Heroes in mythology are created
by a culture in answer to its particular ideology or needs. People assess the gods as color equivalents or electromagnetic field
forces. Myths are the projection of human wisdom and in-
stincts into "colorful" tales about heroes who once lived and

became ennobled, sanctified, and haloed. Some tales reveal the directional drift and unconscious response of man to archetypical patterns associated with color. Myths reflect the wisdom of a race in healing itself with devices of which it may not even be conscious.

The ancient peoples of Tibet, China, Greece, and Egypt seemed to have been more conscious of their bodies than modern man is. They seemed to have also had an inner knowledge of the beneficial effects of the various colors. The ancient Egyptians, for example, built temples for the sick that were bedecked with color and light. They set aside special colored rooms as sanctuaries where the sick could be bathed in lights of deep blue, violet, and pink. Using these finer colors, the patients could attune more peacefully into themselves.

Native American Indians also used color for healing. They used it to fight chronic illness and to heal injuries sustained during buffalo hunts and intertribal warfare.

The Use of Color by the Church

In medieval Europe, color was considered one of the more vital symbols for healing. It was fundamental to most religions. When Europeans wore a specific color, it was not for purposes of attractiveness, but to attune to the divine spirits of the universe.

Color had many religious overtones in the West. The Church, in fact, has traditionally used symbolic colors for ceremonial clothing. White is the color of extreme joy. Purple, along with black, is the color of extreme mourning. Purple combines the warmth of red with the coolness of blue to produce harmony and balance. Icons and religious paintings of the ancients depict figures with haloes or radiating light energy around their heads. This is a recognition of energies beyond those we normally see. Priests and other religious authorities considered these energies in terms of color.

In early and medieval Christian art, every color had a mystic or symbolic meaning that the Church gradually sanctioned. At first, artists and decorators were careful to strictly observe this symbolism, but during the Renaissance, great patrons of art, such as Pope Julius II, gave considerable latitude to such celebrated artists as Michelangelo and Raphael. Hence, the religious tradition became so intertwined with the aesthetic and social traditions that the three are often inseparable.

White

White is sometimes represented in Christian art by silver or diamond coloring. Its chief religious sentiment is purity, as in the Fifty-First Psalm: "Wash me, and I shall be whiter than snow." Early Christian artists depicted God the Father robed in white and Christ after the Resurrection also in white. The Virgin often wears white in pictures of the Immaculate Conception. To denote virginal innocence, white lilies appear in paintings of the Annunciation.

Red

Red, the ruby color, indicates both moral and immoral passion. In its good sense, it is a symbol of divine energy and love, and of the creative power of the Holy Spirit. In its bad sense, it is a sign of hate and of energy that has gone wrong and resulted in cruelty, revolution, and bloodshed. In the latter meaning, it becomes an emblem of Satan. Saint Cecilia is sometimes shown with a garland of red and white roses, the red roses signifying the higher spiritual love expressed in classical music and the white roses standing for innocence.

Blue

Blue, the color of the sky, symbolizes divine or heavenly qualities. Sapphire blue is the color of truth and fidelity. In art, Christ and the Virgin Mary are given the blue mantle of everlasting life. As a symbol of immortality, suggesting the passing from this life to the next, it has also become a mortuary color.

Green

Emerald green is often the symbol of hope and growth, and is used in this way in many Christian paintings. To Muslims, green is a sacred color, symbolizing immortality. The Buddha is often painted against a green background to denote the permanent life behind all of man's temporary incarnations.

Yellow

Golden yellow, a symbol of the Sun, signifies the power and goodness of God, and is so used in religious paintings. The halo and aureole of a saint are colored gold to show the light of eternal life. By contrast, a dull yellow speaks of treachery, as in paintings of Judas Iscariot.

Purple

Violet or amethyst indicates the suffering of people who die for the love of God or divine truth. In art, Christ sometimes wears this color after the Resurrection, as does the Virgin Mary after the Crucifixion. The violet color often given to the robes of Mary Magdalene became the color of penitents in general.

Black

Black was used by Christian artists to signify mourning as well as the devilry of Satan and the grim struggle against it. The black that Jesus wears in paintings of the Temptation stands for the enveloping maneuvers of the Tempter. Witchcraft, which was called the devil's work, was also known as the black art.

Pagan Color Symbols

Pagan color symbols often differed from those of the Christians. The druids regarded *white* as a symbol of the Sun and light. Hence, druid priests clad in white sacrificed white oxen to the Sun god.

In the Far East, golden *yellow*, once the symbol of the Sun god, became the symbol of the Chinese emperor. The emperor therefore wore golden ceremonial robes.

Green was a sacred color among the ancient and medieval Egyptians, who wore it as a symbol of hope and of the joy of spring. The Muslims carried this symbolism throughout the Middle East, and the faithful, upon returning from their pilgrimage to Mecca, wear a green turban.

Coming into modern times, the East is becoming Westernized and the West is immersing itself in Eastern philosophy. But the West is reinterpreting Eastern beliefs for its own requirements. Western wholistic medicine is predicated on the best of the East combined with current New Age practices. Full participation by the patient in his healing is standard procedure in wholistic health practice.

THE FIRST MODERN DISCIPLES OF COLOR HEALING

As described in his scientific works on color, *Contribution to Optics, Researches into the Elements of a Theory of Colour,* and *Moral Effect of Colour,* Johann Wolfgang von Goethe in 1810 conducted color research that remains unequalled even today. He proved that if white light is intermixed with total darkness, a whole spectrum of color is created. We live between the darkness and light, and this interspace becomes a color world for us. Color is therefore a property of light through its interaction with darkness.

Rudolph Steiner, the Austrian social philosopher born in 1861, declared that life radiates color. He said that out of illness comes a new consciousness that re-establishes its balance in health and healing. When Steiner died in 1925, he left behind a doctrine explaining life in terms of man's inner nature and positing the belief that man has a faculty for spiritual perception and pure thinking independent of the senses. (Please see Chapter Five for a discussion of the modern concepts of color healing predicated on the teachings of Steiner.)

We have so far discussed color as light that is broken down into wavelengths with different vibratory rates. An object that absorbs all light waves without reflecting any back is designated as black. An object that reflects back all light is called white. Green is seen when sunlight hits an object that absorbs all the colors of the spectrum except green, which it then reflects back.

Every color sends out either high or low vibrations that create a feeling of warmth or coolness. But most people don't think about color very much. They look at a painting or choose a wallpaper without considering the significance of the colors to their psyche (mind) and soma (body). But the people of more ancient civilizations, back before the coming of Christ, had a great appreciation for the healing powers of color.

In the late 1880s and again in 1890, Kurschner editions of Goethe's works were published with an introduction and annotations by Steiner. Steiner had spent seven years studying the Goethe Archives in Weimar, Germany, and was deeply impressed with Goethe's approach to color. Steiner gave a number of lectures on color based on Goethe's work and incorporating the results of his own research.

Steiner is today regarded as a genius. He is variously called a scientist, an educator, a philosopher, a religious leader, and an occultist. But all who read his works on chromotherapy agree that he changed the way the world looks at color and health.

The same as Goethe, Steiner helped establish the physical science of color that studies both what is seen by the naked eye and what is experienced by the body. He went further than Goethe, however, and tried to understand color through the emotions, urging people to increase their perception of what they feel.

For Steiner, color was divided into two categories: colors with lustre (red, blue, and yellow) and colors with image (green, white, black, and peach blossom). The lustre colors have activity, and the image colors have form. He called green, at the midpoint of the spectrum, the image of life; peach blossom or flesh tone, the image of the soul; white, the image of the spirit; and black, the image of lifelessness. People reach sense perception through viewing these images of life, soul, spirit, and death, he said.

Besides seeing man as an air-being who inhales and exhales rhythmically, Steiner's philosophy also saw man as a light-being, unfolding in the light of thought and thinking. Steiner believed that the soul lives in the color between light and darkness and that man lives in the feelings between thought and will. All in all, Steiner felt that *life radiates color, and out of illness comes a new consciousness that re-establishes its balance in health and healing.*

COLOR IN THE TWENTIETH CENTURY

In 1943, a fifty-eight-year-old Danish scientist, threatened with Gestapo arrest and death by torture, fled from German-occupied Denmark and managed to reach the Swedish shore in a small motor craft. British friends secured asylum for him in their country, and he soon left Sweden in a British bomber. The pilot had been instructed to provide his passenger with a parachute and, in the event of an attack by enemy aircraft, to jettison him through the bomb bay. The fugitive, knowing nothing of what might be in store for him, spent the whole flight lying on the bomb doors, which were liable to open at any moment.

The fugitive was given a headset to keep him in touch with the pilot, but the headset neither fitted him nor even worked. Thus, when the aircraft was forced to climb to a high altitude, the fugitive inevitably failed to hear the pilot's instructions to put on his oxygen mask. The pilot, believing that his passenger had understood his order, did not realize that the man was lying on the bomb doors, starved for oxygen, unconscious, and nearly dead.

The fugitive, who did live through this near-tragedy, was none other than the famous scientist and 1922 Nobel Laureate Niels Bohr, the first man to reveal the architecture of the atom and the origin of light with its healing color spectrum.

Atoms of Light and Color

"All rays, including light rays," Bohr stated, "have their origin in the atom. To induce an atom to emit light, however, we first have to convey energy to it. How does one supply an atom with energy? Various possibilities offer themselves. One way, for example, is to use heat. . . . Another method is to expose it to an electric field, or to bombard it with electrons, or even to use light itself for this purpose. . . ." The Sun affords all of these modes of energy conveyance for providing the full color spectrum of light to the inhabitants of the Earth.

Bohr explained further, "An atom cannot give off light outwards as long as the electrons in its shell revolve in their stationary orbits. If we keep in mind that light is a form of energy, and that the emission of light by an atom is therefore always associated with a loss of energy that has to be compensated for in one way or another, it becomes clear that, in a system in which the objects capable of oscillating—the electrons—are kept at a constant energy level, energy—in our case, light—cannot possibly be given off outwards."

An atom will absorb only energy that corresponds to "its nature." The sodium atom, for example, will absorb only an amount of energy roughly equivalent to that of a ray of yellow light. The potassium atom will always show a preference for a quantity of energy equivalent to that of a ray of red light. The hydrogen atom will take in quantities of energy that correspond to the energy value of a ray of blue, red, or violet light.

When an atom receives energy appropriate to its nature, the electrons in its shell are raised into a new orbit that lasts about one-hundred-millionth of a second. When the electrons jump back into their original orbit, the energy that lifted them into the new path is released again. This is the energy that becomes visible as electromagnetic waves and therefore as rays of light and color. "The color of the light emitted," Bohr concluded, "can be easily worked out by means of a simple formula that was enunciated by Johann Jakob Balmer."

Johann Jakob Balmer was a mathematician and physicist in Basel, Switzerland. His formula, developed in 1885, is predicated on the color spectrum of hydrogen. In the course of his studies, Balmer discovered that there is a connection between the various wavelengths or lines of light waves and that the connection can be reduced to a formula, called Balmer lines. This formula aids physicists in deciphering the significance of color vibrations.

THE HISTORY OF COLOR IN THE MILITARY

Since the earliest times, military units have had some sort of standard to serve as a rallying point in combat. Flags were prevalent during the feudal period when noblemen would take along their heraldic banners to identify the force they were leading into battle. A feudal soldier served the colors of his lord just as today a jockey wears the colors of a certain racing stable and an athlete wears his school colors. The term "color" thus came to mean "a military flag."

Standardization in the use of military colors dates back to 1751 when the British Army prescribed that each regiment be limited to two colors: the King's (or national) flag and the regimental flag. The United States Army later adopted this practice. Each American regimental flag had distinctive colors and bore the name of its unit. The Stars and Stripes was not used as the national color in battle until shortly before the Civil War; in its place was a blue silk flag on which the arms of the United States were embroidered.

Tradition was responsible for colors being carried into battle long after the improved accuracy of weapons made the custom almost definitely suicidal. The British Army last carried colors into battle at Laing's Nek (1881) during the war in the Transvaal. The United States Army last carried them into battle at San Juan Hill (July 1, 1898) during the Spanish-American War. Military colors are now displayed only at ceremonies.

According to strict military usage, a color is the flag carried by dismounted (foot) units, high commanders, and certain general officers. Only regiments and separate battalions have authorized colors. A standard is a flag carried by mounted or motorized units. The term "ensign" is now used for flags flown on ships, small boats, and aircraft.

HISTORICAL COLORS IN CUSTOM, SPEECH, AND HERALDRY

Historically, colors played a vital part in advancing the speech of primitive man, customs of varying cultures, heraldry from feudal times, and modern social practices and idiomatic talk. The interpretation of color symbols, often obscure, can be traced to the meaning of colors in magic and religion. The seasons have partly Christian-partly pagan symbols. The colors for Christmas are red and green; for Easter, light blue and pink; for

Saint Valentine's Day, red and pale blue; for Saint Patrick's Day, emerald green. National flags also have their color symbolism.

An international code of colored flags is used to signal from ship to ship, and the United States Weather Bureau uses colored flags to indicate the weather. In certain sports and shows, a blue ribbon is given for first prize, a red ribbon for second prize, and a yellow ribbon for third prize.

The English language has many words and phrases derived from color symbolism. Black is found in "a black mood," "the pot calling the kettle black," and "blackmailing" somebody. Blue supplies us with "the blues," "once in a blue moon," "a bolt from the blue," and "a bluestocking." From brown comes "a brown study." Green provides "a green light," "greenhorn," and "green with envy." Pink furnishes "the pink of health," "the pink of perfection," and "the pink of fashion." Purple, dear to the Romans, gave rise to "born to the purple." Red, which can mean both passion and brotherhood, offers the Red Cross flag of mercy and fellowship, "red-letter day," "red tape," "a red herring," and "red-blooded man." White is well known for such phrases as "the white feather," "white as a sheet," and "white-hot anger." The baser meaning of plain yellow can be found in the coward's "yellow streak"; the nobler meaning of golden yellow in the Biblical "golden bowl."

In feudal times, heraldic officials used nine symbolic colors to emblazon armorial bearings. Yellow or gold meant honor and loyalty; white or silver, faith and purity; red, courage; blue, piety and resolution; black, grief; green, youth and vitality; purple, high rank; orange, strength and endurance; and violet or amethyst, passion and suffering. These colors probably derived their meanings from the color symbols of Christian art.

COLOR IN MAGIC, SUPERSTITION, AND SYMBOLS THROUGH THE AGES

From time immemorial, men have used colors in magic, with superstitions, and as symbols of abstract ideas. The ancient Greeks believed that the color of an herbal drink helped to cure the disease. Anglo-Saxon metrical charms show that old English tribal doctors had similar beliefs. The Hellenic tribes imagined the Earth to be composed of four elements—earth, air, fire, and water—and believed that earth is green, air is yellow, fire is red, and water is blue.

Colors also played an important role in medieval magic and superstition. Probably the most famous example is the philosopher's stone, which all alchemists sought in the belief that it would cure all diseases plus turn base metals into gold. A little known fact is that the alchemists were convinced that this wonderful stone was colored red. Red is also a favorite curative color in more recent superstitions. Indonesians say that a piece of bright red coral will keep its owner's teeth in good order. Other people believe that a person owning a ruby will live to a ripe old age.

Since man has never had any general education in the power of color, the influence exerted by it on the lives of human beings all through their time on Earth probably has been accomplished subconsciously. Without actually knowing why, man has been utilizing color in magic, superstition, and symbols through the ages.

The potency of color is everywhere. Color has an effect on almost everything: situations, circumstances, beliefs, opinions, the present, and the future. Look at red again. Its chromatic power is most apparent when a person hemorrhages, as, for instance, in this description of a heart transplant from *Taking Heart*, the book by A. C. Greene:

> There is a feeling of drama when the overhead surgical spotlights are switched on, illuminating the stage where the operation will take place and leaving the rest of the room in semi-darkness, the way the theater takes on its sudden, mystical aura when the house lights go down and the stage lighting takes over the audience's suspended comprehension. The stage is small, no bigger than the human chest. Whether the curtain is going up or coming down depends on which side of it you are on. It goes up for the group of masked individuals, it comes down for the unseen individual upon whom the play is about to be performed. The stage is small, but the drama is the biggest in the world. It is the battle between life and death. The curtains of anesthesia close

in, and the final act begins. . . . Masked and faceless worshippers gather around the altar, uniformly clad in the paper suits called scrubs. The surgeon's heads are encased in close-fitting caps of cloth, with wide masks across nose, mouth, and chin. . . . Along with the institutional greens or tans, rather rapidly a different color can and will be added to the scene when the chest is opened and removal of the organs is begun, and some artery may suddenly give a pop and spray color all over the cast. . . . Red. Blood. The most powerful color the human race is heir to.

3.

Color and Its Effects on Body and Mind

Visible light and color undoubtedly influence and affect living things—plants, animals, and assorted microorganisms. Indeed, virtually every species in the plant kingdom thrives on visible light and is inhibited by infrared and ultraviolet energy. Infrared and ultraviolet at either end of the spectrum, plus the colors located within the visible spectrum, bring about physiological and psychological effects in animals and human beings.

In this chapter, we will explore the effects of color on human psychophysiology, the mental/emotional/physical state of being. We will also discuss what your favorite color says about you.

THE PSYCHOLOGICAL EFFECTS OF COLOR

Hayden Frye, the coach of the University of Iowa Hawkeyes football team, hasn't lost a home game in many years of coaching at that college. Part of his success he attributes to the colors of the home team and visiting team locker rooms. The Hawkeyes' locker room is painted blue. The visiting team's locker room is decorated in pink. The color blue gives the Iowa players a feeling of strength and aggression. Pink, on the other hand, has a weakening effect on physical strength and causes the release of norepinephrine in the body and brain. Norepinephrine is a chemical that inhibits the specific hormones that contribute to aggressive behavior. Frye's paint job therefore diminishes the aggression and strength of the opposing team members.

In 1979, researchers at the University of California at Berkeley concluded a study done within the California prison system. Prison guards selected for their strength and endurance were instructed to exercise with heavy dumbbells. They performed as many curls with the weights as possible. Some of the guards were exceedingly muscular and strong.

One guard was able to repeat the curling exercise with heavy weights an astounding twenty-eight times. When he finished, a tall, wide blue poster board was placed in front of him, blocking his view of everything but the blue color. Even though he felt some fatigue and used the same weights, he was still able to repeat the exercise and even increase his number of curls by one—to twenty-nine curls. However, when the researchers replaced the blue poster board with a pink board, the muscular guard, even after resting, was able to curl the weights only five times. Other strong and musclebound guards repeated the exercise with the same results.

The California prison system has now installed pink-painted "sedation cells" for tough and unruly prisoners. When a prisoner breaks the rules, becomes overly aggressive, or requires disciplining for some other reason, he is moved to one of these pink cells for at least thirty minutes. Hostility, aggressive behavior, and general violence seem to begin decreasing within about ten minutes.

Alexander G. Schauss, Ph.D., the director of the American Institute for Biosocial Research in Tacoma, Washington, was the first to report this suppression of angry, antagonistic, and anxiety-ridden behavior among prisoners. Says Doctor Schauss, who is also the editor-in-chief of the *International Journal of Biosocial Research*, "Even if a person tries to be aggressive or angry in the presence of pink, he can't. The heart muscles cannot race that fast. It's a tranquilizing color that seems to sap your energy. Even the colorblind are tranquilized by pink rooms."

The sedating and muscle-relaxing effects of pink are now being tried by behavioral psychologists on geriatric patients, adolescents, and those in family therapy.

Other colors have been used in prison settings to induce very different results. *U.S. News and World Report* journalist Nicholas Daniloff reported his experiences while being interrogated by the Russians in the mid-1980s. For two weeks, overseas reporter Daniloff underwent psychological torture by the KGB, the Russian secret police. Interred at Moscow's Lefortovo prison, he endured psychological torture involving lockup in a cell painted black to induce depression. Many people find black very depressing. The unconscious associations with black include death, dying, bad investment, terrorism, and treachery. Daniloff admits that the color of death and dying made him more malleable to his KGB interrogators, but he actually had very little to reveal.

The bad effects of black, however, are reversible. London's Blackfriar Bridge was frequently used for suicide. When the black bridge was painted green, suicides there decreased by almost 34 percent.

PHOTOTHERAPY FOR SEASONAL AFFECTIVE DISORDER

In 1986, my wife and I visited the Pribilof Islands (Fur Seal Islands) in the Bering Sea, 225 miles north of the Aleutians and 300 miles southwest of Kuskokwim Bay, Alaska. The Alaskans we met there spoke of the unusually long nights and exceedingly short days.

Beyond the Arctic Circle, around the time of the winter solstice at December 21–22, the Sun does not rise at all for at least one full day. Moreover, at Point Barrow, the northernmost community in the United States, the Sun fails to show for sixty-seven days. It's dark there nearly the entire winter season. During this time, many Alaskans are struck by a syndrome called seasonal affective disorder (SAD), which dramatically alters their attitudes. SAD is a persistent mental illness marked with anxiety, neurosis, and depression every fall and winter, followed every spring and summer with joyfulness, mental peace, tranquility, and psychomotor activity accompanied by much excitement.

The depressive symptoms of SAD often are debilitating and include excessive sleeping (as much as twenty hours daily), fatigue, lack of energy, carbohydrate craving, and weight gain. Furthermore, some women manifest SAD in the form of seasonal premenstrual syndrome (known medically as late luteal phase dysphoric disorder), but only in the fall and winter. These women remain virtually asymptomatic during the spring and summer. Four SAD researchers—Barbara L. Parry, M.D.; Norman E. Rosenthal, M.D.; Lawrence Tamarkin, Ph.D.; and Thomas A. Wehr, M.D., all at the clinical Psychobiology Branch of the National Institute of Mental Health in Bethesda, Maryland—reported on this seasonal premenstrual syndrome occurrence in the June 1987 issue of the *American Journal of Psychiatry*.

SAD, in fact, focuses on this one sex; it occurs predominantly in women and usually begins in early adulthood. In winter, most of these depressed patients will respond positively within two or three days when exposed to bright colors and artificial light every day for two to six hours. However, they will relapse into the syndrome within two or three days if the colors and light are withdrawn.

The idea of using bright spectral colors and light to treat human seasonal affective disorder came from studies with animals showing that changes in the length of the day (the photoperiod) trigger changes in mood, behavior, and physiology in many species. Light waves enter the body through the eyes and travel along the neural pathways first to the hypothalamus (a higher brain center) and then to the pineal gland. The pineal gland is a pea-sized mass of tissue attached by a stalk to the posterior wall of the third ventricle of the brain, deep between the cerebral hemispheres at the back of the skull. The pineal gland secretes melatonin, an important chemical signalling agent causing target sites in the animal to respond in a seasonally appropriate manner. Color and light tend to modify the pattern of pineal melatonin secretion.

Chronobiologists (scientists who study cycles as they relate to biology) have discovered that the pineal gland is a master controller of physiological processes. Its neurohormone melatonin helps it regulate circadian rhythms. Chronobiology studies suggest that the stimulation of pineal glandular excretion provides safe and effective phase readjustment and helps accelerate the return to normal from the symptoms of SAD. Such readjustment support can come from colored lights or from pure melatonin taken as a food supplement.

Studies in the northwestern United States have shown that people can be cured of SAD by using special full-spectrum lights placed in their homes and automobiles. As long as they use these lights, their symptoms of seasonal affective disorder will disappear.

The further discovery that bright artificial lights with colors can suppress human nocturnal melatonin secretion suggests that the retina of the eye, the hypothalamus, and the pineal gland all work together as one mechanism or axis that helps the brain make judgments about the seasons. A person will react with changes in mood, behavior patterns, and personality according to the amount of pineal melatonin his body has secreted.

Some researchers additionally asked, "Does the eye solely enter into bringing about the correction or is the skin somehow involved as well?" Four other psychiatrists, led by Thomas A. Wehr, M.D. (one of the SAD researchers), all from the Psychobiology Branch of the National Institute of Mental Health, attempted to unravel this puzzle. Their medical journal article "Eye Versus Skin Phototherapy of Seasonal Affective Disorder," in the June 1987 *American Journal of Psychiatry*, revealed that the antidepressant effects of phototherapy were much greater for ten out of twenty patients when light was applied to the eyes than when it was applied to the skin. The visual response to color and light is therefore more important for a person to benefit from a ray's healing effect. In their article, Doctor Wehr and his associates wrote:

Light and color administered during daylight hours is an effective treatment for seasonal affective disorder even though it does not extend the apparent length of the day and does not alter the pattern of nocturnal melatonin secretion. . . . In this study exposure of the eyes to light was associated with an antidepressant effect that was superior to that of exposure of the skin to light.

On the basis of this and previous experiments we now know some of the properties of phototherapy that are essential for its therapeutic effect and some that are not. Intensity and duration appear to be important fac-

tors. As we have seen, light applied to the eyes is much
more effective than light applied to the skin. This finding strongly suggests that exposure of the eyes is a necessary condition for the response in most patients, but
it does not rule out the possibilities that light with spectral characteristics different from the ones used in this
study might have antidepressant effects when applied
to the skin or that a subgroup of patients might respond
when their skin is exposed to the light used in this
study. Time of day of treatments is not a critical factor,
although it may influence the magnitude of patients' responses. With regard to this variable the present study
corroborates the finding that phototherapy administered only in the evening is effective. Interruption of
sleep is not a necessary condition. The wavelengths of
light that are necessary for the antidepressant effect of
phototherapy are as yet unknown.*

This National Institute of Mental Health study, along with
other studies, shows that our mental health, even-tempered
personality, socially acceptable behavior, and general efficiency
in life depend to a great extent on normal color balance and
full-spectrum light being maintained in our daily environment.
Our everyday world completes twenty-four hours under the
spectrum of color rays from light. As our technological society
brings us closer to an artificial, controlled environment and we
use more manmade light sources, we are throwing our psyches
more and more out of harmony. In fact, if we are not careful,
we can get ourselves into trouble without even recognizing it.

As part of his research for color studies, Robert Gerard,
Ph.D., of the University of California at Los Angeles, recorded
test subjects' personal experience with, judgment of, and feelings about different colors. He found red was generally considered disturbing by the more anxious subjects; those having
chronic high tension showed a greater physiological response
to red. In contrast, blue calmed the tense subjects; blue is an assured psychological tranquilizer in cases of tension and anxiety.

In short, Doctor Gerard's psychological research proves that blue produces an increased sense of well-being, calmness, and pleasant thoughts for people, while red causes excitement, arousal, and tension.

Faber Birren, an education researcher from the University of Chicago turned color researcher, wrote many articles and books about the psychology of color (see Appendix II for a few of them). In one of his clinical journal articles, "The Effects of Color on the Human Organism," published in 1959 in the *American Journal of Occupational Therapy*, he discusses a doctoral thesis in psychology written by Doctor Gerard for the University of California at Los Angeles. Gerard had painstakingly reviewed the whole area of influence by light and color, especially red and blue, on human psychophysiology. He had answered the questions:

- Do such hues as red and blue arouse different feelings and emotions in people?
- Do the hues induce correlated changes in the autonomic nervous system, brain activity, and subjective feelings?
- Do the patterns of response correspond to the relative energy of the colored stimuli?

Using red, blue, and white lights transmitted on a diffusing screen with balanced brightness and spectral purity, Gerard had measured his subjects' blood pressure, palmar conductance (palm sweat), respiration rate, heart rate, muscular activation, frequency of eyeblinks, and brain waves. To take these measurements, he used an electroencephalogram, and he recorded the results.

Based on Gerard's studies, Birren concludes that active people in schools and hospitals, including outwardly integrated people, nervous people, and small children, will find relaxation in an actively colored environment. According to Birren, the visual and emotional excitement in the environment will match the spirits of these persons and therefore set them at ease. Attempts to pacify the active through chromotherapy or something similar would only bottle up their spirits to a bursting point.

Birren also suggests that integrated people prefer a more sedate environment. He writes:

> A quiet soul told to wear a red dress or a red tie may by no means respond according to the usual pattern. On the contrary, such boldness may make him increasingly shy and embarrassed. In the case of mental disturbance, however, reverse policies may be necessary. A person with an inordinate craving for bloody red—which might lead to trouble—probably should be exposed to blue in order to counteract his temper. The melancholy person, who is tolerant only of drabness, probably should be exposed to red to animate him, physiologically as well as psychically.

THE PHYSIOLOGIC EFFECTS OF COLORS

Gerard's physiology studies were equally revealing. He recorded that red vibrations increased blood pressure and elevated palmar conductance. He wrote, "Respiratory movements increased during exposure to red light, and decreased during blue illumination." With heart rate, he found no appreciable differences between stimulation by red and blue. But the frequency of eyeblinks increased during exposure to red light and decreased during exposure to blue light.

The following are additional physiologic responses to color supported by scientific data amassed by Doctor Gerard and the many color therapists cited in Chapter Five.

Red

The pituitary gland, which is an endocrine gland, comes into play when a person is exposed to red. In just a fraction of a second, a chemical signal goes from the pituitary gland to the adrenal gland, and epinephrine (adrenaline) is released. The adrenaline courses through the bloodstream and produces certain physiological alterations with metabolic effects. The following reactions begin immediately but may not be noticed for a few minutes or even several hours depending on the health of the individual's homeostasis (the physiological process by which the internal systems of the body are maintained at equilibrium despite variations in external conditions):

- The blood pressure elevates.
- Blood flow speeds up, as manifested by an increased pulse rate.
- The rate of breathing becomes rapid.
- The autonomic nervous system takes over and reactions become automatic.
- The taste buds become more sensitive.
- The appetite improves.
- The sense of smell heightens.
- Males become attracted to yellow-based reds while females become attracted to blue-based reds.

Orange

Being half red and half yellow, orange can be either a classifier color or a declassifier color depending on the lightness or darkness of its shading.

The Wagner Institute for Color Research in Santa Barbara, California, defines a classifying color as "one that holds position or alters appeal so that only a limited number of people will respond positively." In contrast, the Institute defines a declassifying color as "one that moves its position downward and extends appeal to a broader number of people."

As a classifier, orange is a pivotal color for a person making a buying decision. Also in the classifying mode, orange in general appeals to just a limited number of people. As a declassifier, orange moves into another range and appeals to a larger percentage of the population, causing more people to react positively to an orange object or concept.

The physiologic effects of orange are:

- The appestat elevates and the appetite increases.
- Relaxation is induced and the potential for sleep increases.
- The rate of blood flow slows down.
- A sense of placidness, calmness, and security develops when orange is combined with blue.

Yellow

A declassifier with a broad-based appeal, yellow causes the following physiological alterations:

- The electrochemical transference from eye to brain called vision takes place the quickest in the presence of yellow. Yellow is the first color a person distinguishes when he "sees" something. It is also the most complex color for the brain to process.
- Humans have an inherent precautionary reaction to yellow in nature, especially when it is combined with black.
- Yellow gets a quick though temporary response from a subject under stress.
- Yellow adds to stress by preparing a person for flight or fight.
- Yellow-painted rooms cause children to cry more often.
- Yellow surroundings cause allergies to flare more frequently.

Blue

Known to produce a calming effect, a deep and strong sky-blue color (known in hospitals as cardiac blue) is the most tranquilizing color of all. When in a person's field of vision, it causes the brain to secrete eleven neurotransmitters that tranquilize. These hormones are chemical signals that bring calmness to the whole body. They also:

- Slow the pulse rate.
- Deepen breathing.
- Reduce perspiration.
- Lower body temperature.
- Lessen sweating.
- Eliminate the flight or fight response.
- Reduce appetite (very few blue foods exist in nature).

Green

Green is a classifier color. Forest green, hunter green, and similar shades cause an anti-allergic or desensitizing reaction in certain groups of people, such as those who have hay fever. In contrast, greens with more white and less yellow seem to appeal to a wider percentage of the population. Favorable metabolic responses occur inside the body when an individual is surrounded by almost any shade of green. These sophisticated physiological alterations include:

- Blood histamine levels become elevated. Histamine is a compound found in nearly all the tissues of the body and is associated mainly with dilation of the blood vessels and contraction of smooth muscles such as the lungs. It is an important mediator of inflammation and is released in large amounts after the skin is damaged, producing a characteristic skin reaction of redness and a wheal. Histamine is also released in anaphylactic reactions and allergic conditions, and causes some of the symptoms of these conditions.
- Allergic reactions to foods are reduced.
- Sensitivity reactions to monosodium glutamate are lessened.
- Histamine release is inhibited from mast cells and basophils even when stimulated by antigens and other allergy molecules (ligands).
- Mast cells and basophils are stabilized.
- Hypersensitivity to food additives is reduced.
- Distress from eczema, diarrhea, and gastrointestinal disorders is lessened in severity and length.
- Vision chemicals that improve acuteness of sight are produced. The opposite color of exposed internal body tissue (mostly red) is surgical green, a shade that aids the doctor's eye by replenishing his vision.

Brown

Brown is generally considered environmentally sound. It offers a healthy ensphere or enclosure in which to work, play, sleep, and generally perform common metabolic functions. An aggregate of brown things influences the internal organs and mind in an enhancing way. Brown is a homeostatic color and lends a sense of security. The presence of brown helps:

- Dispel mental depression.
- Promote the synthesis of serotonin (a neurotransmitter).

- Reduce irritability.
- Eliminate chronic fatigue.
- Stimulate the formation of prostaglandin E_1. Prostaglandin is a hormone-like substance in the tissues and body fluids. It has many functions, and it factors in the actions of the womb, brain, lungs, kidney, and semen. Brown's effect on prostaglandin E_1 is therefore significant for the body's overall normal functioning.
- Increase tryptophan amino acid levels that influence sleep, migraine headaches, immunity, and moods.

WHAT YOUR FAVORITE COLOR SAYS ABOUT YOU

When you favor one color over another, you are telling a story about your personality and behavior. For example, a person who dislikes all colors is also likely to hate music, children, and the world as a whole, which he believes has done him wrong. Most of all, the color-hater will intensely dislike himself.

Color preferences are innate. You are born with an attraction for particular colors. What you feel about them will probably last throughout your lifetime. Like you, your color choice is the result of your genes, early childhood memories, education, parents' beliefs, cultural training, political leanings, and other aspects of living.

Little children who cannot yet speak whole sentences will often express themselves eloquently with a set of crayons. A general delight in colors shown by an adult is thought by psychologists to demonstrate the normal emotional tendencies of the very young. Children usually love bright colors.

A child's preference for the black crayon probably indicates repressed emotion or strict parental domination. A love of yellow is classified as revealing a youngster's infantile traits and a dependence on adults. Red shows carefree feelings. Green means the child is balanced, with few emotional outbursts and a simple, uncomplicated nature. Youngsters' color representations of their mothers are nearly always with pastel shades and of their fathers with darker shades.

And so it is with adults. A preference for one color over another reveals your true personality—the characteristics of your

Colored Lenses to Correct Dyslexia

To help individuals who have reading- and writing-based problems, 2,000 educators and 42 clinics around the world are utilizing new diagnostic techniques to identify scotopic sensitivity syndrome, a factor in dyslexia.

Dyslexia is an inability to read properly because of a developmental brain disorder that causes the victim to confuse various letters; it is sometimes known as "word blindness." Affecting more boys than girls, dyslexia is different from mere slowness in learning to read and does not indicate low intelligence—some children with the condition are of above-average intelligence. However, dyslexia (pronounced dis lek'see-a) creates serious education problems. Sometimes called specific dyslexia *to distinguish it from acquired difficulties with reading and writing, it is difficult to diagnose (although special tests for children have been devised). It involves perceptual distortions, such as switching words around on the page, reading words backwards, and confusing letters such as "b" and "d." These misperceptions may be present to some degree in one person in twenty, but dyslexia responds to treatment, especially if begun early. One of the corrective treatments can be found at The Irlen Institute in Long Beach, California.*

The institute's president, Helen Irlen, who has a master's degree in education, says, "In the perceptually handicapped, there is a subgroup of people identified as dyslexic who significantly improve in seeing the printed page when they use colored lenses. Or, the dyslexic's correction may be as simple as placing a specific nonglaring colored filter over the printed page. A dyslexic's perceptual processing problem—his or her scotopic sensitivity syndrome—causes distortions of letters, numbers, musical notes, and other per-

ceptual activities. It is impacted by particular conditions of lighting, black/white contrast, and illumination. Perceived distortions affect the ease and efficiency of one's reading as well as the actual ability to learn how to read. Such a person may find that reading is so laborious and painful that he or she avoids reading, does not do well in school, cannot read for comprehension, or avoids reading for pleasure. Of persons having reading difficulties, 40 percent of them suffer from distortions of scotopic sensitivity syndrome."

At The Irlen Institute, dyslexia is effectively diagnosed, and the type of misperception is identified so that an appropriate color may be applied for correction. Corrective lenses are worn in what appear to be sunglasses. The range of colors is limitless because each dyslexic needs his own individual color for correction. For more information, contact Helen Irlen at The Irlen Institute (see "Resources for More Information" on page 167 for the address).

"self" and of the eye with which you see from within (sometimes referred to by New Age enthusiasts as "the third eye"). Following are some of the personality traits associated with the color you adopt as your own.

Red

If you adopt red as your personal color, it shows that you are outgoing. You are assertive, vigorous, and prone to impulsive actions and variable moods. You feel deep sympathy for fellow human beings and are easily swayed. You have a strong sex drive, entertain stimulating fantasies, and would dive into extramarital affairs if a strong sense of duty did not hold you back from acting on your secret desires. You are an optimist, but you are also a complainer and do not hesitate to voice your complaints.

Orange

If you adopt orange as your personal color, you are good-natured, enjoy being with other people, and are swayed by outside opinions. You do good work, have strong loyalties, feel good will, and possess a solicitous heart. However, unwarranted feelings of elation often pervade your psyche.

Yellow

If you adopt yellow as your personal color, you have a well-functioning imagination, nervous energy, neatly formed thoughts, and a need to help the world. However, you tend to be aloof and more given to theory than to action; you are inclined to speak of lofty doings without doing them. Secretly, you are shy, long to be respected, crave admiration for your sagacity, and are a mental loner. You are a safe friend and a reliable confidant.

Green

If you adopt green as your personal color, you are a good citizen and a pillar of the community, "keep up with the Joneses," and are sensitive to social customs and etiquette. You are frank, moral, and reputable. You make a splendid teacher, have a normal sex drive, and feel deep affection for your family.

Blue

If you adopt blue as your personal color, you are deliberate and introspective. You have conservative convictions, retreat to gentler surroundings in times of stress, and are sensitive to the feelings of others. You keep a tight rein on your passions and enthusiasms, are a loyal friend, and lead a sober life. You nourish preposterous dreams but don't act on them. Stupidity in others annoys you, as does superior intelligence.

Purple

If you adopt purple as your personal color, you have a good mind, a ready wit, and an ability to observe things that go unnoticed by others. You are easily incensed and are verbose when witnessing misfortune. You have a degree of vanity, display a fine-arts creativity, and relish the subtle but recognize the magnificent.

Brown

If you adopt brown as your personal color, you perform your duties conscientiously, are shrewd when it comes to money, are obstinate in your habits and convictions, and are parsimonious. You are dependable and steady, disdain impulsiveness, and can bargain as well as any horse trader.

Gray

If you adopt gray as your personal color, you are cautious, try to strike a compromise in most situations you encounter, and seek composure and peace. You have tried very hard to fit yourself into a mold of your own design.

Black

If you adopt black as your personal color, you are above average, worldly, conventional, proper, polite, and regal. Black is a color that means one thing (depression) to the clinical psychologist and quite another (dignity) to you.

MISCELLANEOUS EFFECTS OF COLOR

Diverse interpretations are associated with purple. Purple gives mixed messages. Historically, of course, purple denoted royalty and grandeur in Western European society. Kings, queens, dukes, and other members of the royal family wore it. But the color is also associated with illness. To symbolize vomiting and other forms of sickness, Japanese Kabuki dancers wear headbands of purple.

Red increases the appetite. Some expensive restaurants use red tablecloths and napkins to increase the appetite by raising the metabolic rate. People on a weight control program should stay away from red-decorated restaurants, tomato sauce, and sliced watermelon.

Conversely, people refuse to eat blue-tinted foods. People have a natural aversion to eating something blue. Weight-loss programs are more successful when the meals are eaten while looking at blue decorations.

Ode to the Personality of Colors

Audrey Kargere, Ph.D., a color therapist active three decades ago, was the protege of the famous color healer E. J. Stevens. She also worked with the horticulturist Luther Burbank and studied color intensely as a science. Her 1979 book Color and Personality *contains the following poem that almost summarizes the personalities of the separate colors:*

> *The scarlet flames with passion,*
> *The crimson rays with lust,*
> *The green-blue glows with reason*
> *While murky blue distrust.*
> *The violet-blue for healing,*
> *The cerise of soul spells might.*
> *Orange-yellow is soothing,*
> *While all the colors spell white.*
> *Now white is the symbol of purity and age,*
> *Precious reward for saint and sage;*
> *The inner light in hours of rest,*
> *Color insignia, the best!**

*Audrey Kargere, *Color and Personality*, © 1979 Audrey Kargere (York Beach, ME: Samuel Weiser, Inc., 1979), p. 22. Used by permission.

According to color researcher Faber Birren, yellow stimulates anxiety and is the most irritating color to the retina of people over fifty. It increases blood pressure within thirty seconds. Black brings on a feeling of depression in forty-five seconds. Knowing this helps us to understand how we can influence other people and how, in turn, advertisers, merchandisers, marketers, and industrialists sway us in our thinking and buying habits.

4.

The Subliminal Pull of Colors

he first impression is always the most lasting one, whether you're looking at a person, a scene, or a product you might like to buy. And what is the first thing you see when looking at any of these things? The color!

CLASSIFIERS AND DECLASSIFIERS

As mentioned in Chapter Three, Carlton Wagner, who is internationally known for his unique multidisciplinary expertise in the use of color and its psychological effects, talks about colors as classifiers and declassifiers. People respond to classifiers and declassifiers in predictable patterns, he says.

Orange draws attention quickly, indicates informality, and loudly proclaims that the product is suitable for everyone. Orange is a declassifying color and can turn the look of an expensive hotel, such as the Intercontinental of New York City, into an inexpensive one, such as a roadside motel in upstate New York, because it is seen as a common man's color. Declassifying colors extend the appeal of a product or service to a broader range of people.

Yellow is another declassifier and signals cheapness, temporariness, and caution. Yellow is the color that the eye registers the quickest and the one likeliest to stop traffic or sell a house. Even a single row of yellow marigolds growing outside a home for sale will hasten the payment of a deposit. Since yellow also signals caution, it is preferred for rental cars (Hertz), school buses, and taxis, but not for banks. Splashes of yellow, such as in a bouquet of flowers, are cheering, but a mass of the color tends to increase anxiety and cause tempers to flare. Babies cry more frequently and with greater gusto in the presence of yellow. Temperamental artists, opera singers, writers, and musicians also seem to explode the quickest in yellow rooms.

Forest green and burgundy are classifying colors. These two shades are preferred by the wealthiest 3 percent of Americans. Colors that classify elevate a product's position or target a specific buying population. Giorgio's new perfume "Red" is being marketed in a blue-based red container and is selling with great success. Women inherit a preference for bluish reds, while men seem to favor yellowish reds.

Red, a declassifier, has many virtues. It makes people unaware of how much time is passing and is therefore the color of choice for casinos and bars. Studies show that red makes food more aromatic and entices people into eating more. Even if you shun red cherries because of their red dye, they seem to make a fruit salad in general taste better.

Indeed, all people are sensitive to the color of food. Appetites are quickened or dulled in part because of a food's vividness or dullness of color. Restaurant owners have known how to stimulate the ordering of food by their patrons since 1878 when colorist Edwin D. Babbitt first published his book *Principles of Light and Color*. Vivid red wallpaper, goblets, tablecloths, and napkins tend to make diners outgoing and expansive. Orange and peach colors stimulate the palate in the same way. In contrast, blue, a classifier, diminishes the appetite; people tend to eat less from blue dishes.

The color of clothing is an important factor in swaying the minds of other people. Inasmuch as royal blue conjures up a sense of tradition, responsibility, knowledge, caring, trustworthiness, and authority, it should be worn to win a public debate, negotiate the terms of a contract, interview for a job, participate in a panel discussion, appear on television, or do some similar activity of significance.

"If you have to pick the wardrobe for your defense lawyer heading into court and choose anything but blue, you deserve to lose the case," proclaims modern-day colorist and marketing expert Carlton Wagner. But should a lawyer wear bright royal blue clothing in the courtroom? A female attorney might do well wearing this color, but a man might not. Sex is still a factor in the colors worn. The suit material's texture and pattern are also significant.

"Black is so powerful it could work against the lawyer with the jury," Wagner adds. "Brown lacks sufficient authority. Green would probably elicit a negative response."

What is the opposite of the declassifying color orange? It's gray! A color that moves its wearer upward on the socioeconomic class ladder, gray is a classifier. When worn as a tailored suit or topcoat, it makes a person seem educated, authoritative, and artistic. In his book *The Wagner Color Response Report*, Carlton Wagner says, "Creative people are more creative in a gray environment than any other color tested." Furthermore, he advises, "Other than navy blue, there probably is no other color that is better suited to business wear."

THE PIONEERS OF COLOR USE IN MARKETING

Richard Wedaa, Ph.D., the director of Color Information Systems of Las Vegas, tells how Henry Ford said in 1909, "Any customer can have a car painted any color that he wants, so long as it's black." Today, cars do come in almost any color. A wide range of colors is offered by many paint companies because of the pioneers of marketing who were the first to use color.

Edwin D. Babbitt, a scientist, physician, mystic, and artist, was the unwitting developer of color psychology in marketing. Attempting to heal physical and mental ills through the application of color, he first brought marketing theory to the foreground in a minor way in 1878. But when he published an updated edition of his book in 1896, he won world fame not only as a colorist but also as the originator of color concepts in marketing. Many of his theories were translated into different languages.

Before Babbitt, S. Pancoast worked with colors and simple techniques. For example, he passed sunlight through panes of red and blue glass. To accelerate the nervous system, he used red. To relax it, he applied blue. He attributed many miraculous cures of illness to his methods of color therapy and cited numerous case histories. He believed that white, the quintessence of light, stimulates healthful activity; red, absolute motion; yellow, general activity; blue, repose; and black, absolute rest.

Not content with Pancoast's simplistic techniques and healing concepts, Babbitt developed the termolume, a cabinet with colored lights in which a person could sit for treatments. He also designed the chromo disk, a funnel-shaped unit that localized light and could be fitted with special colored filters. In addition, Babbitt was the one who brought red, yellow, and blue windowpanes into Victorian homes.

Faber Birren wrote of Babbitt's major premise:

> The center and climax of electrical action which cools the nerves is violet; the climax of electrical action which is soothing to the vascular system is blue; the climax of luminosity is yellow; and the climax of thermism or heat is red. This is not an imaginary division of qualities, but a real one. The flamelike red color has a principle of warmth in itself; the blue and violet, a principle of cold and electricity. Thus we have many styles of chromatic action including progression of hues, of lights and shades, of fineness and coarseness, of electrical power, luminous power, thermal power, etc.

Business and industry today recognize Babbitt's work, although they do not directly attribute current public relations and marketing methods to him. For example, the Pittsburgh Plate Glass Company of Florida publishes a sales booklet, *Color Dynamics*, that it hands out at no charge. The booklet's public relations message reads, "Laboratory tests and practical experience prove that there is energy in color which affects your health, comfort, happiness, and safety. By using the energy in color, you can paint yourself a home not only lovely to look at but also lovely to live in."

Doctor Max Luscher, the producer of a broadly-used merchandizing method, explains in his book *The Luscher Color Test* how a behavioral pattern can be determined by the way a person groups eight specific colors to form a sequence pattern.

Marketers employ Luscher's concepts in order to stimulate consumer purchasing.

WHAT MARKETING COLORISTS KNOW
ABOUT CONSUMER PREFERENCES

People generally have color preferences when they purchase consumer goods and services. Marketing consultants who specialize in color are aware, for example, that most Americans pick blue as their favorite color. The next most popular color with American consumers is red, followed by green, white, pink, purple, orange, and yellow.

Pale blue is known to encourage flights of fantasy, and temperature measurements indicate it can actually cool body temperature. There are physiological differences between men and women, and color can be used to take advantage of them. For example, at the same room temperature, a man can feel five degrees warmer than a woman. Therefore, in factories and laboratories with mostly men, industrial color consultants advise that interiors and exteriors be painted blue to save on heating bills. In contrast, places where women are the primary workers should be painted camel because this light brown color produces a warm feeling in women. This latter practice can also reduce fuel bills.

Nature has probably conditioned most people to feel secure and safe around green. Research has documented that people who work in green environments feel stomachaches less often and less severely than workers in areas of other colors. One reason green is the main color in many hospitals, clinics, and operating rooms is this tendency to reduce pain and other discomforts.

Faber Birren applied his color research to practical industrial purposes. For instance, in 1935, the manufacturer of billiard tables for basement rumpus rooms, a company then named Brunswick-Balke-Collender, found that most American women would not accept the green-topped billiard table into their home because they associated its color with cheap pool halls and gambling dens. As an industrial color consultant, Birren recommended changing the color of the table covering to a soft purplish tone. The Brunswick-Balke-Collender Company complied, and home sales of the purple-topped table skyrocketed.

Brown is a good color for marriage counselors, private investigators, newspaper reporters, and others who depend on interviewing for gathering information. Color consultants advise that brown is a symbol of informality and invites people to open up through conversation. However, according to Carlton Wagner, brown products do not sell well in locations with a large elderly Jewish population. "My research shows that they may resist this color as a hangover from Hitler's brownshirts," Wagner says. An exception is terra cotta, a brownish-red color not associated with the persecution, hate, religious prejudice, and other tribulations of the Holocaust.

In merchandizing, yellow elicits the quickest response from potential purchasers. It stops traffic, looks good, and acts as a kind of magnet for those seeking a bargain. It denotes low price, tentativeness, and cheerfulness. Yellow kitchens help cooks cook better; however, they can also produce high anxiety in others. Yellow is a better color for pass-through areas, such as foyers, hallways, elevators, and laundry rooms.

The simplest color for the eye to process is gray. It is a classifier color that inspires creativity, enhances artistic appreciation, and symbolizes success. On the other hand, people reared in bleak areas, such as the treeless landscape of Sudbury, Ontario, or the coal mining area of Beckley, West Virginia, have a learned bias against gray. Also, noncreative people see gray as a dirty or grimy color.

White has long been associated with goodness, such as white-hatted cowboys and the white knights of the Round Table. People dressed in white are seen as exemplifying purity, chastity, cleanliness, delicacy, refinement, and formality. The nurse in white is believed to be more competent than a nurse in any other color uniform.

Black, conversely, is associated with bad, harmful, and scary things, such as the black arts, witches, and demons. It has mysterious and nether-world connotations. Still, black also signifies dignity, sophistication, refinement, power, believability, and authority. It is the correct color for the chairman of the board's suit, but not for that of a junior executive. Marketers know that black will sell automobiles, but it won't sell airline tickets. Passenger planes are usually white or silver, but never black.

Plastic food wraps are now coming in various colors. Books, cleansing tissues, and paper towels are also being offered in a range of colors to appeal to a variety of buyers. But marketers who experiment with new shades could cause manufacturers to pay dearly for their mistakes. For this reason, marketers now first study the human metabolic response—the physiological reason for how and why people react to a color.

Corporate Color Associations

Many of America's most profitable and best-known corporations have employed color to improve their image, their profits, or both. For instance, General Motors Corporation reports that when a trucking or construction company looks for a truck featuring durability, reliability, and power, it buys one in black or dark brown; these are the best-selling truck colors. Indeed, *Forbes Magazine* reported that an individual's personality is reflected in the color of his car. Automobiles painted red or yellow represent a bold, adventuresome personality; gray, silver, and light green mean moderation; dark blue and black reflect a "touch of class"; and earth tones, light blue, green, and gold reveal practicality in the owner.

Doctor Richard Wedaa says, "Italians love conservative grays and yellows for their cars—they hate using any other colors. The Swedish like blue—it gives them that 'touch of class.' The British prefer reds, blues, and white for their cars. The favorite colors for compact cars [in the United States] are red, light red/brown, white, light blue, and dark blue. In the mid/full-size cars, the favorite colors are light red/brown, white, dark blue, light blue, and gray/silver."

Porsche automobile dealers contend that they sell more cars in red than in any other color.

The Holsum Bread Company increased its product sales by changing its bread wrappers to the "edible" color of red-orange.

Society associates a dove gray color with high socioeconomic status, intelligence, and quick decisions. Upper-income people are attracted to gray. Knowing this, the Sharper Image Corporation, a company that sells high-priced toys and other luxuries for adults, decorates its stores, located in shopping malls, in dove gray from floor to ceiling. Marketing research performed for the company indicated that this color would help to sell more merchandise.

Many corporations now hire color and light experts to create the right conditions for their employees. Everything a person sees or touches has a color to it, and that color must advance the company's or industry's goal.

The power of color in business and industry is characterized by three main objectives for the workplace: improved communication among workers, reduction of workers' stress, and increased work productivity. There are also some secondary gains from achieving happiness among workers by the use of color: reduction of fatigue, elevating the standard of living, and better health for everyone in the company.

Marketing Airline Travel With Color

The power of color was confirmed in marketing, psychology, physiology, safety, recreation, and business when three major airlines took wing in May 1989 with looks redesigned mainly around color. All three airlines wanted to market their services to more passengers. Their chosen color combinations focused on red.

USAir unveiled its new red-white-and-blue plane design at airports in Washington, D.C.; Pittsburgh; and Charlotte, North Carolina. It wanted to trade in its small-carrier look, according to the May 14, 1989, issue of USA Today. After acquiring Pacific Southwest and Piedmont Aviation, USAir had doubled its number of domestic passengers. Its new color design includes a red stripe along the length of the plane, a dark blue tail with three red stripes, and a white USAir logo.

In Tokyo, Japan Airlines rolled out its sleek, remodeled airliners—with the stylized initials JAL and a bright red square. The planes now feature the JAL acronym in black brush strokes. The red square symbolizes the "burning enthusiasm of youth," and a gray band denotes "vibrancy and speed."

Northwest Airlines, in Minneapolis, showed off its new airplane image colors—red, gray, and white. It gave up its patriotic color scheme, but retained its distinctive red tail, a trademark from World War II when its planes crossed the Arctic Circle. If a plane crashed in the frozen north, suggested John Diefenbach of Landor Associates, the San Francisco-based designer firm that created the JAL and NWA designs, the red color could be easily spotted. It's red for rescue.

In assimilating to Asian culture, however, several American airlines have made some blunders. For example, when United Airlines began its concierge service in Tokyo, it had its people wear white carnations to identify themselves as United employees. But in Japan, white symbolizes death and mourning. United had to switch to red when the mistake was pointed out to its executives.

IBM Guards Its "Big Blue" Trademark

The International Business Machines Corporation (IBM) has put a lock on the color blue as part of its industrial logo. IBM is so jealous and protective of the positive image its nickname "Big Blue" projects to consumers and the corporate world that it sought and received a trademark for the nickname in 1988. The color blue elicits a highly emotional response from IBM's corporate boardroom members and executive management.

Proof of this emotionalism came on May 8, 1989, when Jeffrey Alnwick, owner of a small computer equipment company, Big Blue Products Inc. of Northport, New York, received legal notice from IBM that he had thirty days to drop "Big Blue" from his company's name. Alnwick had used "blue" as part of his company's name for six years. He said he never meant to profit from IBM's good name and did not compete for the same markets. In fact, he said, many of his clients—mainly office supply dealers in rural New York, Vermont, and Maine—never even heard of the IBM nickname and repeatedly asked him why he chose such an offbeat business name. He said he always explained that he had once worked for a computer company in Tampa, Florida, called the Big Blue Corporation, which had gone out of business. IBM had never complained about that company, Alnwick added, even though they had had contracts together.

"We're concerned that this will confuse the public and harm IBM," said "Big Blue" spokeswoman Rita Black in 1989. She explained that IBM's nickname derives from the color of the mainframes it sold in the early 1960s. If Alnwick's company failed to comply, Black declared, IBM would take "appropriate action," namely a lawsuit.

Giant "Big Blue" IBM had a worldwide work force of 387,112 people in 1989. In contrast, tiny Big Blue Products had five employees. "No one's ever confused us with IBM," Alnwick said. If he would have to change his company's name, the company would be ruined, the small business executive predicted.

With a groan in his voice, Alnwick tried to explain to IBM why he needed to retain "blue" in his business name. "IBM thinks I should roll over," he said, "but I've got kids to put through college."

In the past, IBM has lost two similar cases on technicalities. This case is currently unresolved. However, IBM will continue to jealously guard its "Big Blue" trademark.

COLOR REACTION TIME

Marketing psychologists advise that a lasting color impression is made within ninety seconds and accounts for 60 percent of the acceptance or rejection of an object, place, individual, or circumstance. Because color impressions are both quickly made and long-held, decisions regarding color can be highly important to success.

Carlton Wagner says, "Your response to color is inherited, and it is learned. Response depends on several factors including your sex, age, intelligence, and education. Also such factors as temperature, climate, socioeconomic background, and regional attitudes will affect color response."

As your status in life alters, your color preferences adapt to your new circumstances: the current fad, your social group, your income level, your home, and your professional standing. The speed of your response changes over time, too.

THE EMOTIONAL IMPACT OF COLORS ON THE PALATE

What color cake icing do most people hate? Most people hate blue icing because it makes them feel queasy.

Which two colors elicit good feelings in people occupied with meal planning, food shopping, food preparation, cooking, eating, or serving? The most pleasing colors to the palate are white and brown.

Conversely, which two colors do potential diners find unappetizing, distasteful, and possibly even revolting when associated in any way with food packaging, food appearance, or meal presentation? Always blue and frequently black.

People smack their lips at the thought of white food products, such as ice cream, milk, yogurt, cottage cheese, coconut, mashed potatoes, marshmallows, fresh fish, rice, and meringue. They enjoy dining with white tablecloths, white napkins, and white china, and being served by white-jacketed waiters. People associate white with mother, her breast milk, and the succor she once gave. Restaurants and food specialty shops would do well to change their decor to white to suggest comfort, security, wholesomeness, good nutrition, cleanliness, and other consumer emotions that benefit businesses purveying food.

Imagining brown foods, such as broiled steak, chocolate cake, hot coffee, walnuts and almonds, whole grain wheat, baked beans, and fresh-baked sourdough rye and pumpernickel breads, makes people salivate and feel hungry. People enjoy these foods in part because they are brown, and they like the color brown during dining in part because they enjoy these foods. There is an easy association between the color brown and the natural, probably because the earth and the bark of trees is brown. Also, broiled, baked, and fried foods are usually brown. Market research has proven that naturally brown foods packaged in brown containers tend to be purchased very readily. In addition, when brown is combined with white for decorating a restaurant, supermarket, or food shop, the appetite is stimulated and sales increase. One reason Brown Cow Yogurt sells exceedingly well in health food stores is that it not only turns out a highly nutritious product but also has "brown" in its name and brown coloring on its container.

But could you picture yourself eating blue spaghetti, blue beets, blue cantaloupe, or blue cereal? Yuk! Never! It's unappetizing and inhibiting. Put a blue spotlight in your kitchen and you'll suddenly have a terrific means of achieving weight control. Blue tends to discourage people from eating. They don't swallow much food from blue dinner dishes, which is why a restaurant's "all-you-can-eat blue plate special" is so cheap. While seafood restaurants can get away with a blue decor, blue-colored steak houses and vegetarian restaurants find it difficult to stay in business for very long.

Black, however, is different from the other three food-related colors. Unlike blue, which doesn't function well at all, black as a background for food works somewhat well when combined with white as a neutralizer. And there are some black foods, such as Spanish olives and licorice, that people generally like. But for the most part, black's association with death and mourning suppresses the appetite and reduces the pleasure of eating. For this reason, food is seldom served on black plates or on tables covered with black cloths. However, waiters and maitre d's can wear black, but black on them is not meant to enhance the appetite of patrons. Rather, black clothing is worn by servers to build up their power and dignity; it gives the head waiter a certain hautiness.   .

Contrary to what black does, red encourages people to eat greater quantities of food and to linger over it for longer periods of time. Diners enjoy red-checkered tablecloths, red wallpaper, and red crockery.

Green vegetables combined with foods of other colors make everything on the plate look more appealing, especially if the table is covered with a green tablecloth. The greenness of the vegetables appeals to the emotions and makes the diner feel healthy and close to nature. Even folks who don't like lettuce admit that a bowl full of salad is comforting and attractive.

Interestingly, the molecular structure of the color green makes all green foods an antidote to sweets such as white crystalline sugar, artificial sweeteners, angel food cake, honey, and candy. Green makes the sweet taste feel cloying to the tongue.

In antithesis, pink makes a food's sweet taste more enticing. People eat more sugar-coated goodies (baddies?) in pink surroundings, from pink food packages, and looking at pink decorations such as streamers and other party favors than when surrounded by any other color. The emotional pull of pink can make you fat.

COMMUNICATING YOUR IDEAL IMAGE THROUGH COLOR

Would you like to charge a higher price for your services? If so, make burgundy a part of your image. Upper-class men and women are attracted to blue-based red tones, of which burgundy is one of the most apparent. However, burgundy discourages the purchase of products and services by the lower socioeconomic class. Lower-class people are even unlikely to buy a hamburger and fries from a stand painted burgundy. This rich color produces uneasy feelings in low-income people.

Lincoln green, or forest green, is also an upper-income color. It gives status to products such as costly automobiles and indicates that services may be pricey but worth it. "The best" is forest green's status indicator.

If you want to be noticed, wear blue-green. It causes contrasting reactions in men and women, but both sexes will respond to it. Men are attracted to women wearing blue-green clothing in the same manner that they are drawn to prostitutes. Men tend to be sexually influenced by blue-green clothing because it makes them think the woman is an easy conquest. Women should be warned that men undervalue women in blue-green garments. Conversely, women instinctively like the color on other women and react positively to the wearer.

THE PSYCHOLOGICAL POWER OF COLOR MARKETING

The power of color comes from light, especially sunlight. The marketing psychology of color is tied directly to the brain's supply of melatonin neurohormone and how it responds to light (see Chapter Three). Edwin D. Babbitt wrote in his book *The Principles of Light and Color*:

> Light being an actual substance moving with peculiar styles of vibrations according to the particular colors

which compose it, and at a rate of nearly 186,000 miles a second, it is easy to see that it must have great power, and that the substances receiving it must partake of this power. The fact that the whole world, mineral, vegetable and animal, is ever being transformed into new and beautiful growths, forms and colors under its magic touch, shows its almost omnific power.

In summary, color is that aspect of the appearance of objects and lights that depends upon the spectral composition of light reaching the retina of the eye. The psychological power of color marketing is dependent upon the variations of this spectral composition in space and time. Generally, the term "color" refers to what is seen and so is an aspect of the visual perception of human beings. From its various psychological effects that have aspects of other factors—such as physiological, mental, emotional, political, financial, sociological, and mechanical factors—color builds its power to sway thinking, change actions, cause reactions, and affect the fate of events. It can be said that destiny is tied to color.

In chemistry, color means simply dyes and pigments. In physics, it relates to spectral composition. In psychophysics (the study of physical stimuli and the perception of physical magnitudes), color influences the variations of what is seen.

Color receives and returns radiant energy that can act as either growth-factoring nourishment or damaging cellular poison. The power of color is indisputable.

THE LOVE/HATE RELATIONSHIP WITH COLORS

Some people will walk into an office or home and immediately hate its colors. Because of this effect on them, these people feel uncomfortable and most likely either will not be good company or won't do their job well. Is there a mental or psychological barrier involved in this love/hate relationship with colors? Decidedly yes! A person's dislike for a color can affect his performance at work, at play, and in social relationships. It can also affect him in more subtle ways, such as by producing stress in his internal organs. The effects can be merely annoying or downright devastating, but they can be overcome.

If you relate a certain color to a negative experience in your life, a simple way to offset that color's negative effects is by studying its opposite color. For example, you might hate the color red because it was once involved in a bad situation that caused you extreme anger or upset. You are now involved in a similar situation. To move beyond the previous negative experience and face the current circumstance with a more calm and relaxed frame of mind, you should think of blue, which is the opposite of red.

People prefer certain colors because interior designers get together every year to decide which colors should be popular during the forthcoming 365 days. The designers use the term "fashion," and nearly everyone prefers to be fashionable; consequently, the general population will follow the trends set by these interior stylists. However, most folk cannot or will not redecorate their homes or offices every year. Redecorating costs a lot in money, time, and inconvenience. The best way for the average person to enjoy colors in his home and office, therefore, is to find the three colors he likes the best and work the "trendy" or "fashionable" colors around them. The decorating costs won't be so high, and he can still keep up with the trend.

Doctor Wedaa suggests that people should always know their sensitivities to colors. "If you love red," he says, "you belong in the midst of life. If you love blue, you have a secure hold on your future. Blues, reds, and greens are what most people prefer. Red is positive, blue is tranquil, and green is the color that balances both of them."

Colors also indicate a person's interest in the world. If a person wants to have a winsome manner or a cheerful personality, states Doctor Wedaa, orange is the color to wear. Yellow is better worn when a person is seeking greater self-fulfillment. A preference for blue/green combinations indicates a discriminating person who draws attention from both sexes for varying reasons. Excitable people usually wear shades of blue to calm themselves down.

Although colors have both positive and negative interpretations, if you take away the restrictions of style and stay with your favorite colors, using other colors just as accents, you will invariably feel good about yourself. It's worth the effort. And by making the effort, you will become a healthier person.

5.

Healing With Color

The history of medicine studies the history of man's health and diseases since the beginning of recorded time. It shows that the goals of medicine have always been to promote good health, to prevent disease, to restore health, and to rehabilitate the patient. Healing with color as one of medicine's modalities reaches all of these goals.

Color has been administered as a therapeutic modality since prehistoric times. In this chapter, we will discuss the many methods of healing with color, its roots in folk medicine, and the high-tech applications currently being tested in research programs.

Color has been adopted as a remedy for illness by shamanists, occultists, natural healers, homeopaths, psychic healers, nurses, naturopaths, chiropractors, optometrists, health educators, modern physicians, traditionally trained clinicians, diagnosticians, hospital personnel, medical center administrators, wholistic therapists, and even dentists and podiatrists. Color therapy, in fact, is finally becoming an accepted and established part of clinical and medical office settings. Most health professionals around the world who practice on the cutting edge of advanced medical techniques—especially those utilizing methods of nontraditional and complementary medicine, such as visualization and imagery, orthomolecular nutrition, acupuncture, biofeedback, and electromagnetics—are aware of the power of color for healing.

COLOR IN FOLK MEDICINE

Disease is a dynamic process that develops in all people. The disease process dates back before man and was coincident with the first form of life on this planet. While not as old as disease, healing approaches began with Neolithic man, who started civilization when he cut and polished the first stone. Colors were a main part of man's nostrums from about 12000 to 4000 B.C., when the archaic cultures of Sumer (an ancient non-Semitic society of Babylonian origin), Egypt, India, and later China made their appearances. Sources for research are carved stones, folklore, myths and legends, psychoanalytic studies of the "magic thought" of primitive man, and primitive tribes still in existence today.

There were no treatments back then for major diseases and disabilities. Compound fractures, psychoses, and smallpox, for instance, were resolved by killing the patient to prevent his becoming a burden on the tribe. Minor diseases were treated with herbs, massage, poultices, dieting, and spectral colors. All these methods had already become an established part of folk medicine when written records were finally begun in biblical times.

Empiric healers—such as medicine men, witch doctors, and shaman conjurers—were enlisted because they were inspirational and combined the functions of the scientist, magician, priest, statesman, and bard. They possessed and distributed various items they believed would prevent disease, including *fetishes*, which were objects laden with magic powers; *amulets*, objects that protected against black magic; and *talismans*, good-luck objects. Each of these objects was painted or stained a color that held great significance. The color brought its own psychic factor to the patient.

Magic medicine, which lasted several thousand years and was based on the principle of doing no injury to the patient, took into account the psychic motivations for each disease and endeavored to understand them. Often the therapy involved expulsion of the problem through bleeding, purging (vomiting), diuresis (increased urination through the use of a diuretic), and catharsis (increased defecation through the use of a laxative). Not infrequently, the treatment was administered in a room or area of some special color, and the patient wore clothing of the same color.

MODERN COLOR THERAPY

Today, color therapy as an adjunctive healing modality matches a color with three required courses or processes: 1. the various symptoms and signs of illness known to be affected by the color; 2. the specific physiological effects desired and known to be caused by the color; and 3. the individual body parts and organs known to be influenced by the color.

The modern science of applying color as a remedy, antidote, neutralizer, prophylactic, and/or nostrum sprang from the research done by German poet, novelist, playwright, scientist, and critic of life and living Johann Wolfgang von Goethe. It advanced further with the creative help of Austrian social philosopher, anthroposophy founder, educator, editor, scientist, and color therapist Rudolph Steiner. A significant statement in Steiner's philosophy affirms that *life radiates color, and out of illness comes a new consciousness that re-establishes its balance in health and healing.*

Color therapy has now entered the New Age through the experiments of, among others, light researcher, photographer, and author John N. Ott. Even though some states, such as California, wrongly label color therapists as "quacks," even sending them to jail for alleged crimes, the technique of color therapy is steadily advancing. The public wants it because it is disillusioned with allopathic techniques and the toxic side effects of drug therapy. Consequently, doctors and therapists on the cutting edge of progressive healing are making color modalities a part of their armamentarium. In forthcoming years, the techniques of healing with color will become more and more known.

Radionic Research Using Color Therapy

A scientific basis for color therapy was laid in 1979 by Douglas Pratt, Ph.D., of the University of Minnesota. A member of the university's biology department, Pratt had been researching the effect of colored lights on plants. He discovered that very deep red colors and very deep blue colors speed up and slow down, respectively, the metabolism and overall growth of plants. These colors might similarly affect human beings, he suggests. Such medical research has yet to be carried out, however, and Pratt anticipates that investigative work on associated topics will be conducted first on animals and then on humans.

In 1978, William Tiller, Ph.D., chairman of the Department of Material Science at Stanford University, investigated the work of George de la Warr, a radionics researcher in Oxford, England. In his own published works, Doctor Tiller confirms that radionic research using color therapy has merit for human healing and deserves further investigation.

The theory of radionics is that every part of the human body (and of animal bodies, too) radiates a specific level of energy. If all these energies are at their proper levels, the individual's etheric body is in balance. The etheric body is the spiritual essence of the physical body, but it exists in the abstract and is thus nontangible. It carries the spark of life and can be viewed externally as the colors of the aura (see Chapter Seven). If an individual's energy levels are either too high or too low, the etheric body is out of balance or in disharmony. Disharmony in the etheric body can result in disease in the physical body. According to the radionics theory, nothing occurs in the physical body unless it first happens in the etheric body.

Radionics was originally developed in the early 1900s by Albert Abrams, M.D., a San Francisco physician whose hypothesis was that diseases can be diagnosed by evaluating the radiation coming from the body. Doctor Abrams devised a machine, the oscilloclast, to measure this radiation. His work in radionics was never considered successful, but his theories have been refined and expanded by other researchers.

"My experience is that it [the oscilloclast] is very effective in the hands of the right person," Doctor Tiller said during a telephone interview with Gary Stemm, a staff writer for the *Virginia Beach Ledger-Star*. Doctor Abrams has applied the oscilloclast to diagnose variabilities in his patients' auras, which are the rays or layers of colored etheral vapors emitting outwardly from the living body.

Administered to an individual's multicolored aura, which is said to be an electromagnetic field extending out about three feet around the entire body, color therapy restructures a harmony for the person. People with psychic healing abilities (occultists) can be trained to see the multicolored aura. A few say they can even diagnose diseases by interpreting the intensity of each color and the distance each color extends out from the body (see Chapter Seven).

Using radionic principles, a chiropractor, Charles F. Whitehouse of Virginia Beach, Virginia, has developed his own diagnostic machine, the etheronic analyzer. With it, Doctor Whitehouse says, he can measure changes in the concentrations of energy in an aura and the strength of the energy coming from any specific part of the body. By bringing the etheric body's aura back into balance, Whitehouse says, he is able to treat a physical disease. And he says he brings the aura back into balance by shining a specific combination of colored lights on it. He uses different color combinations—white light blocked by colored filters or colored lights themselves—to correct different health problems.

Radionics Healing in Action

Each color of light vibrates at a different frequency. The color vibrations reach the patient's etheric body and "energize it to start vibrating and do what it should be doing," says Doctor Whitehouse. Before treating a person with radionics for any particular illness, the color therapist must first clean out the person's aura in general. This is necessary, he says, because the aura may contain ruptures or leaks. Ruptures can occur in anyone from such experiences as having anesthesia administered, having an accident, suffering an emotional shock, having a high fever, smoking marijuana, taking hallucinogenic drugs, becoming intoxicated from imbibing alcohol, and undergoing any similar form of pollution. In our over-polluted, industrialized world, about seven of every ten people have leaks in their aura, believes Whitehouse. The leaks give vent to disease.

The Virginia Medical Board and the United States Food and Drug Administration (FDA) are investigating Doctor Whitehouse. The FDA became involved as a result of his etheronic analyzer. That agency regulates the use of medical equipment in the United States. Yet, at least three of the chiropractor's many patients have stepped forward to praise his healing techniques.

Janet Whittenberg, a homemaker from Norfolk, Virginia, says she obtained good results for her mentally-impaired three-year-old son, Shannon. "I had gone to so many doctors and hospitals," says Mrs. Whittenberg. "Shannon was a vegetable. He did not do anything. They said his brain was deteriorating, and there was nothing they could do. They considered him a terminal case."

On the advice of a neighbor, she took Shannon to Doctor Whitehouse, who administered color therapy to him.

"I saw results within a month," Mrs. Whittenberg says. "He had only two teeth in his mouth and in one month every tooth came in. He had stopped growing, and he started growing again. He was all yellow but that faded away. Now he is very alert, knows everyone in the family, and watches TV. I am very pleased."

Betty Drury, of Newport News, Virginia, says she has seen "tremendous improvement" in her fifteen-year-old mongoloid son, James, since she began taking him to Doctor Whitehouse for color therapy. "He remembers better, keeps up school work better, writes better, recognizes more words, and his features are changing," Mrs. Drury says. "Before we took him to Doctor Whitehouse, he was very hyperactive, he tore up everything and he couldn't even tie his shoes. After a month of treatment, he suddenly sat down and tied his shoes. And he hasn't torn up anything since. Everyone in the family notices the difference."

Mrs. Drury says doctors told her that James was uneducable and untrainable. But, she says, he is learning more now after having been exposed to the vibrations of the colored lights. "His speech therapist at school is amazed at the difference," she said. "James has started making 100s on every one of his tests."

A third mother from Virginia Beach says she has been taking her brain-damaged six-year-old son to Doctor Whitehouse. "There's been a lot of progress," she says. "I'm encouraged by what I see and very pleased, but I don't know that I'm ready yet to have my name be used." Still, she has continued to take her son to Whitehouse for color therapy because the boy has slowly but steadily been improving. And medical doctors, she says, had told her there was nothing that could be done.

This third mother explained that her son has been suffering from brain damage since birth and could do little more than roll over before receiving the color treatment. Now, she says "He has become aware of his surroundings; he scoots all over the place; he is starting to relate to people and developing a temper. He still can't walk or talk but he can do a lot of vocalizing with sounds."

A Case History of Healing Cancer With the Spectral Colors in Sunlight

Helen Fleming, Ph.D., chief of Radiologic Technology (now Radiography) at Merced Community College in California, was diagnosed in 1982 as having an advanced case of lymphatic cancer (lymphosarcoma). Because of the potential side effects, Doctor Fleming chose not to take the oncologist's recommended X-radiation therapy and chemotherapy. (She was assisting the radiation medical specialist at a nearby hospital and saw almost daily the horrible effects caused by that specialist's ministrations.) Instead, she decided to try the full spectrum of color healing from sunlight.

Accordingly, Doctor Fleming took a leave of absence from Merced College and, with her husband, moved out into the country where she could spend most of her time outdoors taking sunbaths in the nude. Her goal was the absorption of spectral colors. She sunbathed faithfully, and her lymphoma tumor disappeared.

When eventually this radiologic technologist returned to her teaching job in the Department of Radiology and resumed working under ordinary fluorescent lights, the tumor came back. Color and light researcher John Ott, who related this story, was called upon by Doctor Fleming to install his radiation-shielded, full-spectrum Ott-Lite, which simulates sunlight. With ultraviolet (UV) added to her office, classroom, and home,

Doctor Fleming's lymphoma again just virtually disappeared. When she finally did die, it was from a heart atttack and not cancer.

How did full-spectrum light act as a healing agent for Doctor Fleming's cancer? The remission of her lymphoma may have occurred because ultraviolet light is known to penetrate the skin to a depth well below the capillary network. Therefore, the blood in Doctor Fleming's capillaries received the same color spectrum ultraviolet treatment it would have from X-radiation but without having to be withdrawn from her, run through a UV irradiating device, and then returned to her bloodstream.

A provocative study on skin cancer and ultraviolet appeared in the August 7, 1982, issue of *The Lancet*. The study was jointly conducted by researchers at the Department of Medical Statistics and Epidemiology, London School of Hygiene and Tropical Medicine, London, England, and at the Melanoma Clinic, University of Sydney, Sydney Hospital, Sydney, Australia. The researchers challenged the theory that sunlight exposure was directly related to the incidence of malignant melanomas. In the published study, the researchers reported finding that there was a much higher incidence of malignant melanomas among Australian office workers than among people who are occupationally and otherwise regularly exposed to the colors in sunlight. Spectral colors in sunlight in fact seemed to protect against malignant melanoma when UV light exposure was routine as opposed to concentrated and sporadic as in suntanning salons or when office workers go on a short vacation once or twice a year.

THE TEN BASIC POSTULATES FOR COLOR HEALING

Whether or not the conventional allopathic physician practicing American mainstream medicine is accepting or even cognizant of color therapy, color is basic to any system of healing. Color is nature's own curative measure, and it functions under certain basic postulates, some of which have already been discussed. The following is a list of ten postulates adapted and expanded from a shorter list originally presented in 1964 by R. B. Amber, of Calcutta, India, in his book *Color Therapy*:

1. All earthly objects, animate and inanimate, have their own characteristic frequency of vibration.
2. All living cells, tissues, organs, and other human body parts have their own characteristic frequency of vibration in health.
3. Illness is an altered physiological functioning that is the body's natural response to stress. Altered functioning is nothing more than a change in frequency, with the stepping up or lowering of the vibration caused by a stressor. The stressor can be from a chemical, mechanical (physical), or thermal source. Mental and emotional stressors help change a frequency when they cause an internal chemical response, such as hormonal stimulation.
4. All illnesses have a characteristic frequency of vibration.
5. Applying a corrective frequency in the form of food, physical therapy, injection, nutrients, oral drugs, exercise, color, or some other eclectic method of healing will help an altered function return to its homeostatic pattern
6. Body cells selectively take in normal rays and vibrations from the environment when they need them. However, if the environment presents overly strong rays and vibrations, the cells will absorb them even when they don't need or want them.
7. Cells that lack color vibrations, the same as cells that lack nutrition, will tend to depolarize and alter their frequencies and, therefore, their patterns of growth. If too much color is present in the immediate environment, cells will overcharge to such a degree that their frequencies and growth patterns will alter to the point of damage.
8. The same as a toxic food, a wrong color can change the electromagnetic force field or frequency of a cell, which sets up a chain reaction: the change of frequency will interact with the larger field of force of the organ, which in turn will affect the body system, which in turn will react upon the total individual. Such a chain of reactions can lead to chronic fatigue syndrome (the new so-called "yuppie disease"). The fatigue may then bring on exhaustion in the organism and eventually death.
9. Color, as pure vibration, is the rational therapy for maintaining health and overcoming disease (as a complemen-

tary or alternative treatment to more traditional allopathic chemical medicine or drug treatment) because it presents itself for the body's use in the right form (or food), in the right place, and at the right time.

10.   Color can be readily adapted for clinical application by physicians who practice orthomolecular medicine.

PHYSICIANS USING COLOR THERAPY

Without color, there is blackness followed by death. With color, there is white light with correct physiological functioning by the human organism. For this reason, original thinkers in medicine now exist who have become unhappy with the standard "Establishment" methods of treatment because, they feel, patients do not recover fully enough from the disease and pestilence besetting them in this modern era. These thinkers include the members of progressive medical academies and the health professionals on the cutting edge of New Age medicine. Many of them believe that cancer and other diseases may possibly be reversed by using the proper color vibrations. Two groups that believe this are the Great Lakes Association of Clinical Medicine, headquartered in Chicago, Illinois, and the American College of Advancement in Medicine, in Laguna Hills, California. (See "Resources for More Information" on page 167 to receive more information on these two groups.)

William Campbell Douglass, M.D., of Clayton, Georgia, is one of these progressive thinkers. While no longer in practice, Doctor Douglass is utilizing ultraviolet irradiation therapy in the form of an instrument he is currently marketing called the Ultra-V (also known as the Photolume). Doctor Douglass' method uses the technique of photopheresis to irradiate the blood of an ill person with ultraviolet to conquer infection, cancer, erysipelas (a streptococcus infection of the skin), rheumatoid arthritis, some cases of autoimmune deficiency disease, including AIDS and ARC (AIDS-Related Complex), thrombophlebitis, and bronchial asthma. It can also be used to improve peripheral blood circulation in the treatment of toxemia, or blood poisoning. (See "Resources for More Information" on page 167 to receive more information.)

Photoluminescense With Ultraviolet Radiation Therapy

In an as-yet-unpublished manuscript on photopheresis (the medical potential of ultraviolet light), Doctor Douglass lists the physiologic actions and effects of ultraviolet energy when its photoluminescense is absorbed by the bloodstream. "The effect is physical, then chemical, and finally biologic," he states. "Photochemical reactions are initiated by change in electronic configuration and velocity. If the incident energy is short enough, it will produce vibrations in the electrons, which will then be activated. These electrons may then be ejected and the molecule thus ionized; or they may be displaced to an outer orbit and then the atom or molecule is 'activated.' Photoelectric phenomena are the basis of all the subsequent reactions."

According to Douglass, the following reactions take place in the human body when ultraviolet energy strikes it:

- Calcium metabolism is profoundly improved by an increased blood content.
- Bacteria in the body are killed by the direct action of the UV rays and indirectly by increased local and systemic resistance.
- Toxins in the body are rendered inert.
- Normal chemical balances in the body are restored.
- Cellular imbalance in the blood is corrected if UV is administered in suitable doses.
- Fat elements in the blood that were altered in character by disease are restored to normal size and brownian movement. (Brownian movement is the random movement of small particles suspended in a fluid caused by the statistical pressure fluctuations over the particle.)
- Oxygen absorption is increased following UV irradiation of autotransfused blood.
- The immune system is depressed, immune resistance to bacterial infection is lessened, and the bacteriocidal potency of the blood is reduced with a fall in hemoglobin by an overdosage of UV.

While individuals vary greatly in their sensitiveness to ultraviolet irradiation regarding systemic and skin effects, sensi-

tivity to it is cumulative. Eventual sensitivities may be modified
by certain drugs such as sulfanilamide, particular foods such as
buckwheat, and specific pathogenic substances such as hema-
toporphyrins. The action of ultraviolet may be immediate,
somewhat delayed, markedly delayed, or protracted on any individual. Ultraviolet irradiation acutely illustrates the power of
color on all people.

HEALING COLORS FOR CERTAIN DYSFUNCTIONS

Besides the unseen color of ultraviolet, which spectral colors
are useful in the treatment of which pathological conditions?
Colors are most readily applied to a specific dysfunctional human or animal body part or organ in the form of colored lights.
Various shades of each color are employed by therapists depending on the strength of the physiological effect required.
The application of the lights utilizes techniques similar to those
of Doctor Charles F. Whitehouse. However, the lights are
placed directly at the site of the pathology to gain the appropriate therapeutic response from the dysfunctional tissue, cell
structure, organ, or body part.

The following is a list of the healing colors and which
bodily dysfunctions they treat.

Red

Red stimulates the sensory nerves, so it benefits the senses of
smell, sight, hearing, taste, and touch. It activates blood circulation, excites the cerebrospinal fluid, and rouses the sympathetic nervous system. Hemoglobin is built with red rays. Red
rays produce heat that vitalizes and energizes the liver, the
muscular system, and the left cerebral brain hemisphere. As a
muscle relaxant for contractures, red's counter-irritant effects
are excellent for therapeutic purposes.

Red decomposes the body's accumulated salt crystals and
thus catalyzes ionization. The ions created then carry electromagnetic energy throughout the body. The rays split ferric salt
crystals and liberate heat.

Known disorders treatable with the color red include:

Anemia
Asthma
Blood dyscrasias
Bronchitis
Constipation
Endocrine system dysfunction

Listlessness
Paralysis
Physical debilitation
Pneumonia
Tuberculosis

Conditions contraindicated for using the color red include:

Emotional disturbances
Excitable temperament
Fever
Florid complexion
Inflammations

Hypertension
Mental illness
Neuritis
Red hair

Yellow

Yellow activates the motor nerves and generates energy for the muscles. A disturbance in the supply of yellow vibrations to any part of the body can bring about a disturbance of function there, including partial or full paralysis. Yellow, as a mixture of red and green rays, has the stimulating potency of red vibrations mixed with the reparative potency of green vibrations. Therefore, it tends to both stimulate function and repair damage.

Directed at the gastrointestinal tract for short periods, yellow is a digestive aid; for longer periods, it acts as both a catharsis (purge) and a cathartic (laxative). It helps to eliminate parasites and worms, and stimulates the flow of bile.

Nerve building takes place in the presence of yellow. It has a stimulating, cleansing, and eliminating action on the liver, intestines, and skin. It energizes the alimentary tract, purifies the bloodstream, activates the lymphatics, and depresses the spleen. It lifts despondency and suggests joy, gaiety, intellect, perception, and merriment.

Known disorders treatable with the color yellow include:

Arthritis and rheumatism
Constipation
Diabetes

Digestive problems
Eczema
Exhaustion

Flatulence   Liver disease
Hemiplegia   Mental depression
Indigestion   Paralysis
Kidney disease   Paraplegia

Conditions contraindicated for using the color yellow include:

Acute inflammations   Heart palpitations
Delirium   Neuralgia
Diarrhea   Over-excitement
Fever

Orange

Orange combines red and yellow rays, and its heating power is greater than that of either red or yellow alone. Orange stimulates the thyroid gland and depresses the parathyroid. It expands the lungs, has an antispasmodic effect on muscle cramps, aids calcium metabolism, acts as an emetic, and increases the pulse rate. But orange does not affect the blood pressure. Milk-production in the breast is stimulated after childbirth when a new mother wears orange clothing. Orange also acts on the spleen and pancreas to help assimilation and circulation.

Known disorders treatable with the color orange include:

Asthma   Kidney ailments
Bronchitis   Menstrual difficulties
Colds   Mental exhaustion
Epilepsy   Prolapsed uterus
Gall stones   Respiratory diseases
Gout   Rheumatism and arthritis
Hyperthyroidism   Tumors, both benign and
Hypothyroidism   malignant

Conditions contraindicated for using the color orange include:

None known

Green

Green—both dark and pastel—builds muscles, bones, and other tissue cells. It is neither acid nor alkaline, and can be used the same way blue is used. Green is cooling, soothing, and calming both physically and mentally. It relieves tension, lowers blood pressure, acts as a hypnotic upon the sympathetic nervous system, dilates the capillaries, and produces a sense of warmth.

Green rays help stabilize the emotions and stimulate the pituitary. They can be used for their aphrodisiac quality and for sexual tonicity. The vibrations of green disinfect against bacteria, virus, and other germs.

Known disorders treatable with the color green include:

Asthma	Laryngitis
Back problems	Malaria
Colic	Malignancy
Erysipelas	Nervous disorders
Exhaustion	Neuralgia
Hay fever	Over-stimulation
Heart problems	Syphilis
Hemorrhoids	Typhoid fever
Insomnia	Ulcers
Irritability	Venereal disease

Conditions contraindicated for using the color green include:

None known

Blue

Blue vibratory rays increase the metabolism, build vitality, promote growth, slow the action of the heart, and act as a tonic on the body in general. They have antiseptic properties, contracting potencies for muscles and blood vessels, and a soothing or cooling effect on inflammations.

Blue is the balancing and harmonizing color that returns the bloodstream to normal. It reduces nervous excitement, is astringent, and can be absorbed from the environment during meditation and spiritual expansion. It relaxes the mind. It helps the introvert come out of his shell and comforts the manic-depressive. But after ten minutes of concentrated treatment with blue rays, mental depression tends to set in; blue clothing and furnishings sometimes make a person feel tired.

Blue is the color of truth, devotion, calmness, sincerity, intuition, and the higher mental faculties.

Known disorders treatable with the color blue include:

Baldness
Biliousness
Bowel irregularity
Burns
Cataracts
Chicken pox
Cholera
Colic
Constipation
Diarrhea
Dysentery
Epilepsy
Eye inflammation
Febrile diseases
Gastrointestinal diseases
Glaucoma
Goiter
Gonorrhea
Headache
Heart palpitations
Hydrophobia

Hysteria
Insomnia
Itching
Jaundice
Laryngitis
Measles
Menstrual difficulties
Poliomyelitis
Renal (kidney) disease
Rheumatism (acute)
Scarlet fever
Shock
Skin diseases
Syphilis
Tonsilitis
Tooth infection
Typhoid fever
Ulcers
Vomiting
Whooping cough

Conditions contraindicated for using the color blue include:

Colds
Gout
Hypertension
Muscle impairment

Paralysis
Rheumatism (chronic)
Tachycardia

Indigo

Indigo is electric, cooling, and astringent. It is a parathyroid stimulant, a thyroid depressant, a blood purifier, a phagocyte builder, and a hemostatic agent (it reduces or stops excessive bleeding). It promotes muscular tonicity, respiratory depression, and hypnotic-like insensibility to pain.

Indigo rays control the psychic currents of the subtle spiritual bodies. They also control the forehead chakra and influence vision, hearing, and smell on the physical, emotional, and spiritual planes.

Known disorders treatable with the color indigo include:

Appendicitis	Hyperthyroidism
Asthma	Mental illness
Bronchitis	Nasal diseases
Cataracts	Nervous ailments
Convulsions	Nosebleed
Deafness	Obsession
Delirium tremens	Palsy
Dyspepsia	Pneumonia
Ear diseases	Respiratory diseases
Eye diseases	Throat diseases

Conditions contraindicated for using the color indigo include:

None known

Violet

Violet stimulates the spleen, upper brain, and bones. It depresses the lymphatics, heart muscle, and motor nerves. Violet is calming in cases of mental illness. It controls irritability, reduces hunger, builds leucocytes, and maintains ionic balance, especially of potassium and sodium. Leonardo da Vinci said, "The power of meditation can be ten times greater under violet light falling through the stained glass window of a quiet church."

Known disorders treatable with the color violet include:

Bladder problems	Concussion
Bone-growth dysfunction	Cramps (abdominal)
Cerebrospinal meningitis	Kidney disease

Mental illness   Scalp diseases
Nervous disorders   Sciatica
Neuralgia   Skin diseases
Rheumatism (acute and   Tumors (benign and
  chronic)   malignant)

Conditions contraindicated for using the color violet include:

None known

Ultraviolet

Ultraviolet has chemical and bacteriocidal properties that break down bacterial toxins. Ultraviolet light, at the extreme end of the color spectrum, accelerates the lymphatic and circulatory systems, antibody production, glandular activity, and metabolism. It enhances the action of the lungs, heart, and sympathetic nervous system.

Known disorders treatable with the color ultraviolet include:

Goiter   Rickets
Gonorrhea   Syphilis
Heart disease   Ulcers
Respiratory diseases   Wounds

Conditions contraindicated for using the color ultraviolet include:

Malignant melanoma and other skin cancers

The diseases and conditions listed above as being healed or affected by specific colors are only a sampling. They are the disorders that have been verified as being highly responsive to color treatment. Advanced techniques work wonders on an additional myriad of disorders.

ADVANCED COLOR THERAPY

Sunlight includes a broad spectrum of rays. The ones that tan are the ultraviolet rays (UVs), and they pass directly through the outer layers of the skin to affect the more sensitive lower layers. In addition, there is scientific confirmation that they travel beyond the skin into other parts of the body to produce either a healing or destructive effect depending on which form of UV is predominant.

Two basic types of ultraviolet radiation reach the Earth. Ultraviolet B (UVB) rays are shorter and are the primary cause of sunburn. Ninety percent of their effect is on the skin surface; 10 percent is underneath. The tan a person gets on his skin surface from UVB rays helps to protect against sunburn underneath his skin surface. Ultraviolet A (UVA) rays are longer. They do 90 percent of their damage on the supporting inner layers of skin and have at least ten times the wrinkling effect as UVBs. The tan obtained from UVA rays does not protect against sunburn (as is often erroneously claimed by tanning salons). However, both UVA and UVB rays have both negative and positive photochemotherapeutic effects on human physiology and pathology.

Photochemotherapy

The head of the Department of Dermatology at Yale Medical School, Richard Edelson, M.D., and his colleagues at the General Clinical Research Center of Columbia-Presbyterian Medical Center, New York City, recently employed a technique of advanced color therapy called photochemotherapy. They used ultraviolet irradiation of a drug to make the drug more effective in the treatment of cancer.

Doctor Edelson's article, "Treatment of Cutaneous T-Cell Lymphoma by Extracorporeal Photochemotherapy," in the February 5, 1987, issue of the *New England Journal of Medicine*, reports on significant improvements in patients with lymphoma cancer after they received ultraviolet A (UVA) light and 8-methoxypsoralen (8-MOP).

The 8-MOP was made from natural substances found in lemons, limes, and several fresh vegetables, including celery, parsnips, and parsley, and was given orally to the patients. A half hour later, a quantity of blood was withdrawn from a vein in the left arm of each patient. An irradiating device was used to treat the blood with UVA, and the blood was then returned to the patients but through a vein in their right arm.

By itself, 8-MOP did nothing against the lymphoma. It was the UVA-irradiated blood containing 8-MOP molecules that was the actual chemotherapeutic agent. Edelson and his colleagues report that when 8-MOP/UVA blood was injected, there was a loss of viability in the target lymphocytes. That is, the lymphocytes involved with the cancer cells reduced their activity by 88 percent.

Edelson had previously reported obtaining similar results when he and his colleagues used essentially the same treatment protocol on cutaneous T-cell leukemia in 1983.

Edelson's experience with 8-MOP may explain why amygdalin (laetrile), which is made from natural substances found in apricot pits, works better in sunny Mexico and Southern California than at the Mayo Clinic in overcast Rochester, Minnesota, during mid-winter. Because there was no irradiation of the laetrile, the Mayo Clinic's trials failed and may have erroneously discredited the therapeutic effects of amygdalin.

In Part IV of his series of articles published in the *International Journal of Biosocial Research*, John Ott describes the work of George R. Prout, Jr., M.D., and his colleagues from Massachusetts General Hospital. Prout and his group used a drug for photodynamic therapy by activating it in the patient's body using the colors in spectral light. They wanted to destroy cancer cells in the bladder without harming the normal tissue. Their experiments were conducted in the Peoples Republic of China. Ott writes:

> Similar applications of this approach, called photodynamic therapy, have been used to treat tumors of the lungs and esophagus as well as recurring breast cancer.
>
> Doctors first inject patients with a drug called hematoporphyrin. After waiting two days, the physicians shine light on the cancerous cells in the lining of the

bladder. The light excites the hematoporphyrin that remains in these cells. This kills the cancer cells but spares normal cells, which don't contain hematoporphyrin.

The doctors use a slender fiber tube to get laser light to the cancer. It is pushed through the urethra into the bladder. The laser gives off light but not heat.

"Tumor cells are unable to rid themselves of this compound," says Doctor Prout, who directed the study. "Other cells seem to pass it on very simply." Thus, once again, photochemotherapy or photodynamic therapy uses light with its attendant colors as a healing agent. Personal, societal, and other behaviors are also affected by colors.

The director of the Serammune Physicians Laboratory of Vienna, Virginia, Russell Jaffe, M.D., Ph.D., a Fellow of the Health Studies Collegium, in his clinical journal article, "Immune Defense & Repair Systems: Clinical Approaches to Immune Function Testing & Enhancement—Part 3," published in the *Townsend Letter for Doctors* in May 1990, discusses the importance of one's skin covering in immunology. Doctor Jaffe writes, "The use of sunlight is known to enhance activation of 1,25 DiOH-cholicalciferol (active vitamin D_3), an important immune modulator and calcium regulator, to enhance maturation of the B-lymphocytes [producers of antibodies] and to stimulate connective tissue synthesis."

Speaking in print with fellow wholistic physicians and other health professionals who apply innovative biologics rather than pharmaceutical products for enhancing their patients' health, Jaffe advises that thirty to sixty minutes of full-body exposure to the Sun taken daily gives optimum clinical effects. For example, there is a direct beneficial interaction between antioxidants such as beta-carotene (the precursor to vitamin A) and sunlight exposure. He reveals that wholistic physicians at the Princeton Brain Biocenter in Skilman, New Jersey, find dichromatic lights, particularly green, helpful when sunlight is unavailable. He adds that dichromatic light gives the best results clinically when used as described on page 98.

Among the beneficial effects observed are substantial reduction in galvanic skin response (GSR), a general index of autonomic, adrenergic arousal, after 15–20 minutes use. The effect of light on free radical formation in skin has been studied. The beneficial effects of increased illumination on calcium absorption is reported. Others find enhanced illumination helpful in seasonal affective disorders.

More is not necessarily better and classic wisdom teaches the importance of balance of sunlight and nutrient availability. Light, as radiant energy of particular frequencies does entrain the brain through nonvisual pathways and influences endocrine biological rhythms.

Photobiological Colored Lighting to Produce Immunoregulation

During the day, certain brain rhythms are maintained by fluctuations in light intensity and spectrum. Recent research has linked mood changes to seasonal and circadian fluxes. Other studies suggest that seasonal depression may be reduced by exposure to appropriate lighting sources.

The Sun produces a spectrum of colors generated by refraction. Most mechanical sources produce color by pigment subtraction. In contrast, dichromatic sources, which are the most suitable for photobiologic effects, use materials of differing refractive indices to generate color.

Both visual and nonvisual pathways in the body are employed by physicians on the cutting edge of new advances in medicine for achieving photobiological homeostasis of immunoregulation. These biologic innovators are probably thirty years ahead of the usual traditionally practicing, Establishment-type allopaths stuck in the medical mainstream, as represented by American organized medicine. Doctor Russell Jaffe is one of those biologic innovators. His interest in the mechanisms of health and the evoking of the human healing response led him to apprentice in the systems of various cultures, including such healing arts as acupuncture, meditation, and a variety of related therapeutic approaches. In addition, Jaffe did innovative studies of platelet and other blood cell biochemistry and metabolism. Among the tests he developed are the early colon cancer screening test using occult blood detection not interfered with by vitamin C consumption and a variety of tests related to the blood clotting and immune defense systems. He developed the first method of measuring cell-mediated immunity, which provides an "immunologic fingerprint."

In an explanation of how to apply photobiological colored lighting to produce immunoregulation and advantageously trigger brain rhythms, Jaffe offers the following description:

> The person sits four to six feet from the face of a green light for 20 minutes twice daily. This is typically done in the morning and early evening. A socket-clamp light holder can facilitate positioning of the color source. During this time other activities (such as deep breathing, relaxation, reflex, guided imagery, range of motion exercises, certain reading) can be performed simultaneously. The person need not look directly at the light. Deep brain structures and chemical pathways can be health-adapted by this action.
>
> If indicated, yellow, amber, or blue dichromatics can be arranged to shine on the back, chest, abdomen, or any other specific area of the body. The same position and time conditions apply. Several lights can be used simultaneously. It is best if these are the sole source of illumination. The PAR 38 DICHROMATIC 150 WATT Spot or Flood lights would be the light source. In the United States both Sylvania and General Electric produce these items. Quality lighting suppliers, particularly those specializing in outdoor or theatrical lighting (where true color rendering is important), should carry or be able to obtain these lights for you.

For information on contacting Doctor Russell Jaffe, see "Resources for More Information" on page 167.

THE SEVENTEEN PRINCIPLES OF ADVANCED COLOR THERAPY

According to medical color therapists, there are seventeen principles of color healing. Not one of these principles calls for the use of chemicals alone, as is ordinarily done in the allopathic prescription of chemotherapy. Rather, adjunctive color, as was furnished by the UVA light in the photochemotherapeutic study reported by Doctor Edelson, is the better method of treatment with color and chemicals. Color is the most absorbable and easiest element for utilization by the body because its vibrations are so easily accepted by human tissues.

The application of color for ushering in good health, emotional stability, and spiritual elevation is made most effective by utilizing these seventeen principles.

1. Color can be introduced into a person through colored foods; solarized (exposed to the Sun) liquids and solids; sunlight or "artificial" sun rays applied to the skin; contrasting-colored room decor; colored clothing; birthstones, crystals, and gems; meditation on and in color; colored lights; and color breathing, which changes the consciousness of an individual and helps him reach his aura or electromagnetic force field. (See "Color Breathing" later in this chapter.)

2. Either supply color that the ill person lacks or reduce color that is overabundant and imbalancing to the body. Or, neutralize the overabundant color by furnishing its complementary shade.

3. The two foundation colors of color healing are red and blue. All other colors are subsidiaries or refinements of red and blue. This was independently confirmed by Doctor Douglass Pratt, of the University of Minnesota's biology department, in his research on the effects of colored lights on plant metabolism.)

4. Apply colored lights at the most strategic time and in the most suitable manner to the human body systems, organs, parts, tissues, and cell structures.

5. The purer the color, the more penetrating the rays and the faster the body's reaction.

6. When in doubt, undertreat rather than give too much color treatment.

7. Don't overload one body system to help another. For instance, be careful not to overload the circulatory system

with the eliminating toxins produced by invading micro-organisms when treating an infection.

8. Overexposure to one color can be remedied by applying the complementary color (see principle number 2).

9. If the wrong color is accidentally used, first neutralize the wrong color with its complementary color; then treat the condition itself with the correct color.

10. When planning color therapy either for yourself or someone else, take into account the circumstances under which the treatment will be delivered. For instance, you may need to apply the color as white light behind a color filter. Other circumstances to be considered could be the color medium, any sensitivity of the patient, the quality of the color filter, the nature of the disease, the extent of the pathology, the present weather, the climate, the color needed, the time of day, the season of the year, and the patient's biorhythm. (A biorhythm is a biologically inherent cyclic variation or recurrence of an event or state, such as the sleep cycle, circadian rhythms, and periodic diseases.)

11. Natural color is a more powerful healer than the color in glass, filters, and dyes. It is the power to transmit color rather than the visual effect of color that is important in healing.

12. Misapplied color can deteriorate certain body parts. For instance, misused bright red color shocks the eye, leads to fatigue, and generally irritates. A red room raises the blood pressure; a green one lowers it.

13. Color rays absorbed through the skin affect all the glands, blood cells, and chemicals in the body.

14. Colors in clothing and hair dyes affect the entire body.

15. Artificial light, such as that from an incandescent bulb, and natural light from the Sun both heal by stimulation, oxidation, metabolic enhancement, and immunoregulation.

16. Healing with color aims to reestablish body balance and release tension caused by color starvation.

17. Apply color to a specific organ by first selecting the organ's appropriate trigger points and then the trigger

points' appropriate colors. (See "Trigger Points and Their Treatment Colors," later in this chapter.)

COLOR BREATHING

To benefit from an alteration in electromagnetic forces from imbalance to harmony, the technique most effectively employed is to meditate while performing color breathing. The technique of color breathing, developed by Indian yoga masters, is accomplished by concentrating on the desired color mentally, using it in your respiration process, and meditating.

The best time to practice color breathing is immediately following or preceding breakfast or dinner (not lunch). Color breathing should not be practiced as the last exercise of the night during the first month of employing the technique because it is too stimulating to the mind and spirit. The increase of vital force may prevent sleep. Such controlled breathing not only raises the bodily vibrations, but it unites you subjectively with the Universal Consciousness. You should try to be fully aware during the exercise of the inflow of color rays revitalizing your body and mind systems and replenishing the finer vehicles of personal healing power with cosmic energy.

Procedure for color breathing: Breathe rhythmically from twelve to eighteen times a minute. You might time yourself prior to meditating to establish the inhalation-exhalation pattern. As you respirate in this steady rhythm, you should visualize the colors of the spectrum. If you are attempting to overcome a certain condition, you should use one particular color or its nearest equivalent as your healing agent. Here is the step-by-step technique for correct color breathing:

First, imagine yourself engulfed by a white light from the cosmos that enters your body through your head and moves down to your extremities. See it flood your entire being from within and without. Hold onto this image for at least two minutes.

Second, draw from this spectrum of white light the color specifically required for the healing process you desire to achieve.

Third, visualize red, yellow, and orange being drawn up
from the Earth through the soles of your feet to your various organs. This is the force the Hindus call *kundalini*.

In contrast, visualize blue, violet, and indigo as arriving
from the atmosphere. You should see these colors as vertical
rays entering your body through the anterior fontanel and penetrating into the various organs. The Hindus call this atmos-
pheric force *prahna*.

Visualize green as coming into your body through your navel on the horizontal plane.

Fourth, after employing the necessary color, mentally bathe
your body in white light, allowing your entire self to be engulfed in it. White light begins and ends the self-treatment with
color breathing.

The color healer is a deep breather who is conscious of the
Universal Life-Spirit that is around him. The Universal Life-
Spirit lends healing strength. With each deep inbreathing, the
color healer draws in a portion of this power. He does this inha-
lation while consciously feeling the grandeur of being in harmony with the Infinite.

TREATMENT TRIGGER POINTS
FOR ORGANS AND BODY PARTS

A trigger point is an area of the body that when bombarded
with color affects a related body system, organ, tissue, or other
part dramatically and drastically. Some of the vital areas that
act as trigger points include the body's six nerve centers, the
seven major chakras, and some subsidiary chakras, plus the
fontanels of the head, the carotid arteries, and the gluteal-mus-
cle area.

Certain areas of the body are more important than others
when it comes to treatment with color. The most important
treatment points are the nerve centers in the spine and the solar plexus. These are followed in importance by the forehead,
the back of the neck, the chest, and the abdomen. In general,
treatment should be administered to strengthen the human organism as a whole. Sometimes, however, local applications are
indicated.

The chakras are bell-shaped vortices (whirling, eddying areas of power) in the etheric (nonphysical) body. They each have a characteristic color and intersect with the spinal chord at a definite point. They are specialized channels of color force. The individual color of each chakra relates directly to the healing color for the specific body area near to which the chakra is located.

The violet chakram is situated at the top of the head in the region of the pituitary gland.

The indigo chakram is located behind the mid-forehead and controls the pineal body.

The blue chakram lies within the throat and has its base on the thyroid gland.

The green chakram is situated at the cardiac plexus, which is the heart.

The yellow chakram, the golden center, lies in the solar plexus and influences the adrenal glands, pancreas, and liver.

The orange chakram is centered in the spleen.

The red chakram, the coccygeal center, lies at the base of the spine.

The size and configuration of the chakras depend on the individual person and his stage of development in the astral, mental, and spiritual aspects of life. Each chakram absorbs a special current of vital energy through its particular color ray from the physical environment and from the higher levels of consciousness.

In his book *Rise of the Phoenix*, yogi Doctor Christopher Hills points out that we actually store our vital forces on seven levels of our being, the chakras. Doctor Hills says:

> Just as we have seven major ganglia and seven endocrine systems for secreting hormones, so do we have seven vital force centers which are linked with the operation of the seven brains. . . . [Note: According to ancient Indian doctrine, man has sevenfold bodies labeled Organic, Nervous, Etheric, Astral, Mental, Causal, and Buddic that interpenetrate each other because of their discriminating subtle etheric and atomic structure.] Each chakra is spinning at a different rate of vibration called a frequency. The study of these frequencies con-

tinued in ancient India for many thousands of years until the present day. . . .

To control the frequency and the positive or negative spinning of these chakras gives us conscious control over the positive and negative functions of the brain, and thus control over our own destiny. Instead of pumping all our consciousness into electronic computers and engineering more and more complex systems, our next evolutionary step is to learn to become engineers of our own consciousness and of the forces in society which are reflections of our inner worlds. If even a small group of people came together and practiced awakening the total number of cells in the human brain, the energies developed could liberate the enormous potential of mankind for a New Age.

The Trigger Points and Their Treatment Colors

Treatment with appropriate colors should be administered to specific trigger points on the body to achieve the desired healing effect. The following is a listing of the correct therapeutic colors to apply to particular organs and body systems.

The Brain

Using the color indigo, blue, or violet, quiet the blood and the nerves of the scalp, face, back of the neck, and feet in order to calm the brain. To do this, shine a colored light on these head areas. Or, since the brain can also be reached through the eyes, expose the vision for brief moments to the appropriate colored light.

The Heart

Using the color indigo, blue, or violet for soothing purposes, apply color therapy to the chest, primarily over the heart, and then to the feet and arms. To stimulate the blood and nerves, apply orange over these areas.

The Cerebrospinal System

Using yellow and violet, treat the right side of the head.

The Circulatory System

Using dark green for its calming effect, treat the whole body. To invigorate, use grass green; to stimulate, use bright red. If there is no elevated blood pressure, blue can be substituted for green.

The Upper and Lower Extremities

Use red to treat impairments of the muscle structures, except when shock is involved.

The Endocrine System

At the site of the endocrine gland, use green to comfort all the glands. Use yellow first, then blue, to activate them.

The Abdomen and Loins

Using red, orange, and yellow to stimulate the gastric juices, blood, nerves, and peristaltic action of the gastrointestinal tract, apply the colors to the lower back, groin, hips, feet, and abdominal area, especially the navel region. To overcome diarrhea and inflammation, apply blue, violet, and indigo. Treat the epigastrium with blue for psychological disturbances. For trouble in the loins, such as a hernia or intestinal rupture, use the red spectrum. Treat with green for its tonic effect on the general abdominal region; treat with yellow to stimulate the epigastric nerves; and use blue to relax the abdominal muscles when they are cramped.

The Kidneys and Urinary System

Apply yellow to the lower back, groin, loins, hips, and feet.

The Lungs and Respiratory System

Use yellow and violet on the middle of the sternum on a line with the second rib.

The Musculoskeletal System

Apply red rays to the left side of the head.

The Neck and Thorax

Treat them with purple.

The Nervous System

Use violet and lavender to soothe the right and left sides of the brain. Apply grass green for its invigoration effect, and medium yellow and orange for their stimulation effect.

The Skin

Treat local patches of skin with yellow.

The Sex Organs

Use the color indicated for the local area, such as yellow for the ovaries, uterus, testes, and prostrate because they are situated near the kidneys and urinary system.

The Rectum

Treat as listed for the kidneys, with the color determined by the specific condition.

THE TAKATA EFFECT

It has now been proven that color-ray-frequency changes arising from sunspots affect the flocculation index of human blood.

Flocculation is a biological reaction in which normally invisible material leaves a liquid solution to form a coarse suspension or precipitate as a result of a change in physical or chemical conditions. During this biological reaction, the liquid solution may alter its color and become more easily recognizable.

Flocculation tests using human blood serum and special reagents (solutions) are useful in diagnosing liver abnormalities and other aspects of human normal and abnormal physiology (pathology).

During the early part of the twentieth century, Maki Takata, M.D., a gynecologist practicing in Tokyo, discovered how to use the flocculation index and the color change of albumin in blood serum to study the ovarian cycle in women. He found that the flocculation index increased and decreased with the menstrual cycle. Using the Takata effect, a gynecologist could determine if his patient was ripe for impregnation. Thus, the time of ovulation became predictable. Also, Doctor Takata learned, the index remained constant in healthy men. Because other physicians duplicated Doctor Takata's findings, the Takata discovery became an established part of Japanese gynecological science.

In January 1938, however, doctors in hospitals all over Japan discovered that the Takata reaction had changed dramatically among their patients. It no longer was reliable. Doctor Takata expressed shock at the unfavorable results of his medical test and refused to believe the accuracy of these adverse reports from his countrymen. He took the criticism of the Takata reaction personally. But then more reports from around the world came tumbling into his laboratory, and the conclusion he was forced to reach became undeniable: his medical test did not work anymore.

With determination, Doctor Takata set about looking for the cause of this sudden and extreme alteration in his test's accuracy. From his offices in Tokyo, he cooperated with a medical colleague in Kobe, Japan, and soon learned that the flocculation rate in men from these two cities coincided precisely to the minute during the day and during the night. Then other physicians from around the world began participating in the investigation, and all of their combined data pointed to an amazing finding: some outside factors occurring around the world at exactly the same moment were bringing about a biological change in all human blood. The change had produced an altered flocculation index.

What was this phenomenon? Doctor Takata came to believe, and stated publicly, that the Takata effect was derived from outer space. It is extraterrestrial (ET), he said. Hearing his views, many of the gynecologist's colleagues smirked behind their hands and agreed among themselves that "Takata has gone off his rocker. ET, indeed!"

It took seventeen years of concentrated research before Doctor Takata was finally able to prove in 1951 that color-ray-frequency changes in the atmosphere arising from sunspots really do affect the flocculation index of human blood albumin. Today, these color changes are universally known as "the Takata effect."

Publishing a scientific paper in the *Report of the Academy of Sciences of the U.S.S.R.*, Russian scientist Doctor N. Schulz advises that white blood cells are definitely affected by sunspots. Other scientists carrying on Doctor Takata's experiments have shown equal effects from radiation showering the Earth from outer space. The radiation also alters the behavior of inorganic colloids, such as the sedimentation that forms in steam-engine boilers.

John Nash Ott described Doctor Takata's experiments in Part III of his series, "Color and Light: Their Effects on Plants, Animals and People," published in the 1987 Special Subject Issue of the *International Journal of Biosocial Research*. Ott told how a person's flocculation index would be altered by color rays from sunspots no matter where that person stood on Earth. The only location tested by Doctor Takata and his colleagues that showed elimination of the Takata effect was at the bottom of a mine 200 meters underground at Mieken, Japan. Thus, a person's blood index color can be influenced by the electromagnetic vibrations connected to the colors coming out of sunspots. The Takata effect shows how the internal environment of every human body responds to colors throughout the universe.

THE WORK OF JOHN NASH OTT

After a twenty-year career as a successful banker in Chicago, John Nash Ott turned his hobby and lifelong interest in time-lapse photography into a full-time investigation of the ecology of light and color. His research has brought him citations and awards from horticultural, scientific, and medical societies, along with an honorary Doctor of Science degree from Loyola University of Chicago. For a time, Ott worked with Walt Disney himself, doing time-lapse photography. He eventually began his own motion picture company.

Even now in his eighties, Ott writes and lectures extensively on the field of photobiology.

In what many refer to as two breakthrough books, *Light, Radiation & You: How to Stay Healthy* and *Health and Light*, Ott presents his findings on everyday health hazards and what to do about them. Although they have a lot of repetition, the books do warn of the dangers from overuse and under-regulation of modern electromagnetic technology. The author prescribes color as a healing mechanism. The books, which have easy-to-duplicate demonstrations, point out:

- The relationship of color television to cancer.
- Why pink fluorescence can bring on headaches, high blood pressure, and insomnia.
- How such common objects as ionizing smoke detectors, fluorescent lights, television sets, digital watches, and video display terminals can weaken the muscles and diminish the sex drive.
- How colored lights have cured skin cancers, near-blindness, and goiter.
- Why dark-colored sunglasses may provoke illness and eye disease.
- Why hyperactivity and irritability in some children are related to the kind of fluorescent lighting used in the classroom.
- Why full-spectrum sunlight does possess the healthful and healing properties historically ascribed to it.
- How controlled exposure to certain colors can produce, or reduce, aggressive behavior in both human beings and laboratory animals.

More in the Rainbow Than Meets the Eye

John Ott has performed practical experiments and laboratory tests on plants, microbes, and animals, and clinical studies with people that all tend to prove that the kinds of intensities of light to which living organisms are exposed have a great deal to do with their illness and wellness. His linking light, color, and health answers a number of questions that have puzzled scientists for decades. For example, ordinary eyeglasses, sunglasses, windows in homes, and automobile windshields all screen from the eyes most of the ultraviolet that reaches people in natural sunlight. But sunlight deprivation can become a strong obstacle to the healing of sickness in an individual or to the improving of health in someone who unknowingly is suffering the beginning symptoms of subclinical illness.

Ott points out in his dozens of writings and hundreds of lectures that a very definite relationship exists between the colors making up white or natural sunlight and human physical and mental health. He explains that for scientific purposes, the different colors are defined in the terms of a measuring system using the wavelength as a standard unit. Each color has its own wavelength, which determines the color's proper place in the spectrum. Of course, some wavelengths cannot be seen by human eyes since the waves are either longer or shorter than those that are recognized as colors.

Radiation—Invisible Color

Wavelengths shorter than ultraviolet and longer than infrared, each of which the human eye cannot see at the extreme ends of the light spectrum, are called radiant energy. These radiant energy waves—radiation—at each end of the spectrum are capable of penetrating through ordinary types of building materials even in total darkness. Thus, all of us are exposed to radiation, and this has now also become a special study interest of John Ott.

Ott has investigated the electrical dimension of the human body and has demonstrated its electrical field in a simple way by showing that holding a lightning rod or other straight length of metal causes a loss of muscle strength. His working hypothesis is that negative ions give the body energy while positive ions bring on fatigue and even depression. In his presentations, he discusses the negative effects of digital watches, certain manmade fibers such as polyester and vinyl, ionizing-type smoke detectors, certain kinds of fluorescent lighting, video display terminals (VDTs), electronic fetal monitoring equipment in hospitals, and other high-technology items.

The negative effects and destruction to the body's cells from exposure to ionizing and non-ionizing radiation is vast. Radiation is frightening and one of the major causes for the increase in cancer among people residing in industrialized countries. It is also affecting future generations. For pregnant women, for instance, the negative effects from sitting in front of a video display terminal or being exposed to other forms of non-ionizing radiation include miscarriage. Researchers have also found that heavy users of VDTs are more likely to bear children with birth defects than are light users. This electromagnetic force coming from computers is related to the vibratory rays of colors, especially to those in the rainbow and given off by sunspots.

The electromagnetic force derived from computers is the same form of radiation, although less toxic, as that manifested by gamma rays and X-rays in the stratosphere (biosphere). On the scale of electromagnetic-spectrum frequencies, all of the computer's electromagnetic forces lie close to the level of microwaves (as from a microwave oven). Ultraviolet and the rest of the visible spectrum are part of that same biospheric environment as gamma radiation. The electromagnetic spectrum and its vibratory frequencies are given in Table 5.1.

The Light-Color Healer

On the basis of numerous observations, Ott established that light influences the size, number, and rate of growth of tumors in laboratory animals. The results of similar investigations varied under different types of lighting, so Ott now stresses the importance of laboratories including light as a reported variable in their experiments. Ott additionally observed the stunted growth in plants placed near the ends of some fluorescent tubes. He noted that old fluorescent tubes emit more radiation than new ones.

One of the studies Ott helped to conduct at the Environmental Health and Light Research Institute of Chicago showed

Table 5.1.   The Electromagnetic
Spectrum

Vibratory Frequency	Electromagnetic Force*
10^{-15}	Gamma rays
10^{-10}	X-rays
10^{-7}	Ultraviolet
10^{-3}	Infrared
10^{-2}	Microwaves
10^{-1}	FM
10	Short waves
10^{3}	AM
10^{5}	Radio waves

*Visible spectrum not included.

that rats placed in front of a television set shielded with black paper first became increasingly hyperactive and aggressive, constantly fighting with one another, then became extremely lethargic, and finally all died. However, rats shielded with lead from the television tube's radiation all remained perfectly normal.

When Ott added the microscope to his photography equipment, his time-lapse microphotography uncovered a new tiny world of change that no scientist had until then suspected. Ott observed the movements of cells in elodea grass and learned that the cells behave quite differently under different colored lights. Generally, these cells perform in an established pattern when exposed to any natural sunlight condition, but they break the established pattern and display many variations when different filters are used in the microscope light. The cells can be made to move in different directions according to the colors employed; some are encouraged to stand still and neither flow within nor without the intercellular fluids, while others are encouraged to take up new metabolic patterns.

Animal cells will undergo radical changes when the light colors are changed in the microscope. Ott can increase their metabolic activity or kill the cells merely with the application of colored light.

Working with laboratory mice and using various kinds of lighting conditions, Ott learned how to affect the animals physically. Not only does altering light colors cause external physical changes, but it also has a definite effect on a mouse's sex life and life expectancy.

Ott As FDA Radiology Consultant

In recognition of his expertise with color, light, radiation, and health, the Bureau of Radiological Health of the United States Food and Drug Administration (FDA) asked Ott in 1983 to be its consultant. In this capacity, Ott came in touch with a number of color/light-related projects that called for investigation.

Ott's study involving elodea grass uncovered that different colors (different wavelengths of light) affect individual chloroplasts. In the streaming process of the chloroplasts within the cells of the elodea grass, photosynthesis takes place. Chloroplasts are granules that act as the seat of photosynthesis in the elodea cells, but only in those cells exposed to light with its full spectrum of colors.

Ott also showed the importance of the ultraviolet wavelengths on the pigment granules in the pigment epithelial cells of the retina of a rabbit's eye.

Ott published a four-part series, "Color and Light: Their Effects on Plants, Animals and People," in four Special Subject Issues of *The International Journal of Biosocial Research* in 1985, 1986, 1987, and 1988. He summarizes his life's work and challenges certain sacred assumptions in science and medicine. These four papers, the last two before they were published, came into my possession in an interesting way.

John Ott was invited to speak before the Cancer Control Society of Los Angeles during its fifteenth annual cancer convention during Independence Day weekend, July 2–4, 1987. However, he found it inconvenient to attend this meeting and therefore prevailed upon me to deliver the papers for him. (I was already a scheduled convention speaker on "The Healing Powers of Garlic.") Ott mailed his papers to me for that purpose. As it happened, Lorraine Rosenthal, the executive director of the Cancer Control Society, persuaded Ott to attend and read his papers himself. The final two were subsequently published in *The International Journal of Biosocial Research*. (See Appendix I for information on acquiring these papers.)

In the series, Ott describes the Gocio School study that he conducted for five months in 1973 among Sarasota, Florida, children to evaluate light and health. The Gocio School in Sarasota installed full-spectrum, radiation-shielded fluorescent light fixtures in two windowless classrooms that each contained forty-nine students for a total of ninety-eight children. Two identical windowless classrooms containing the same number of children but with standard cool-white fluorescent fixtures were used as controls. The results showed that several extremely hyperactive children with previously confirmed learning disabilities calmed down completely, rapidly overcoming their learning and reading problems, in the full-spectrum-lighted environments. Furthermore, the overall average academic-achievement level of these entire two classrooms of children showed significant improvement. The children responded exceedingly well in many ways—mentally, emotionally, and academically—to the simulated natural outdoor daylight furnished by Ott's lighting fixtures.

Simultaneously, the Sarasota County Dental Society did a study on the teeth of these same children in the two rooms with the radiation-shielded light bulbs. The dentists determined that these children developed only one-third the number of cavities as did the school's other children (the controls), who pursued their classroom activities under the standard cool-white fluorescent lighting.

Another study mentioned by Ott is one he performed with a group of colleagues from the Environmental Health and Light Research Institute of Chicago. These researchers investigated students at the Adjustive Educational Center of the Sarasota County School System, a special school for children with learning disabilities and related problems. This study showed that all the television sets in the homes of these disabled children were giving off measurable amounts of X-ray radiation. When the sets were repaired or discarded, all the children except one were able to return to their regular classes within a few months.

The researchers learned that the one child who showed no response—even when her viewing hours were greatly restricted and she was made to sit way back from the TV set—was sleeping directly on the other side of the wall from the television tube, which was in her living room. Her pillow was actually only a few inches—the thickness of the wall—from the back of the set. The ordinary building partition here afforded no protection from the radiation. When the situation was corrected, this little girl, too, was able to follow her classmates back to the regular school.

Ott also participated in a research project with personnel at the Wills Eye Hospital and Research Institute of Philadelphia. In patients at the eye hospital, certain tranquilizer drugs were causing various side effects in a layer of cells located right behind the rods and cones of the retina. These pigment epithelial cells were thought to have little to do with vision, but what they did contribute toward sight was unknown.

Ott was asked to do a time-lapse microscopic study of the effects of adding different tranquilizers to the growth media for the pigment epithelial cells while the time-lapse pictures were being taken. He used a phase-contrast microscope that showed the details of the cell structure without having to stain the cells with dye. The dye usually employed for staining would also have killed the cells. The greatest contrast and sharpest image through the phase-contrast microscope is achieved by using a monochromatic light (light of a single color). To obtain this, different colored filters are tried until the filter creating the greatest contrasting light is found. The pictures Ott took very clearly showed that the filter color used in the microscope's light source increased the tranquilizer side effects in the pigment epithelial cells. These side effects happened more so under colored light than when the drugs were administered alone, without color.

Money-Saving Applications of Ott's Color/Light Findings

In the past, when egg-laying chickens were kept outdoors and allowed to roam where they wanted, scratching in the barnyard dirt and nesting in any old place, a laying hen was profitably productive for a farmer for a minimum of five years. With today's standard, modern, and so-called "improved" indoor mechanized methods in poorly lighted, windowless buildings, the birds last for only about thirteen months. Then they must be replaced at a cost of $150,000 for a standard 50,000-hen house of egg-layers. However, when the latest type of radiation-shielded, full-spectrum fluorescent lighting fixtures (the "Ott-Lite") developed by John Ott are installed, even the hens in a windowless chicken coop remain at peak production for at least three years.

In addition to extending the laying period of the hens, the full-spectrum fluorescents have also been shown to help the birds eat $19,700 less feed annually per 50,000-hen house; lay 8.5 percent more eggs (about $39,800 of extra eggs as recorded in 1985 dollars); crack 2 percent fewer eggs, thus saving the farmer $20,000; and produce larger eggs, valued at an additional $7,800. Add to this another farm saving of $4,000 in labor costs from not having to debeak the birds (the chickens in adjacent cages no longer try to eat each other alive), and a total of $91,300 in extra profit can be rung up by the farmer with a standard load of chickens.

A final advantage with potentially far-reaching implications for human cardiovascular health is that the eggs produced by hens basking under the full-spectrum, radiation-shielded fluorescent bulbs that furnish the entire complement of rainbow colors contain 40 percent less cholesterol. In other words, when hens are exposed to all the spectral colors, they produce eggs that are more healthful.

Where to Buy Full-Spectrum Natural Light Bulbs

Network, an independent Dover, New Jersey, distributor, markets John Ott's full-spectrum, natural, healthy lights called Vita-Lite by mail order on a national basis. The company also furnishes Neo-White, a special light bulb coated with the rare-earth element neodymium. Neodymium filters out the excess yellow tinge inherent in most incandescent bulbs.

While studying color in graphic arts classes at the Rochester Institute of Technology, Network's proprietor, Daniel Kassell of San Francisco, became convinced that everyone could improve their quality of living by functioning daily under full-spectrum lights. Kassell, a wholistic-oriented nutritionist, reports that either as fluorescent tubes or incandescent bulbs, pure white light sharpens vision, reduces eye strain, and improves "see-ability" by rendering all objects natural-color in appearance. It shows true flesh tones and reveals subtle differences in the actual colors of objects. It delivers correct lighting for precise color matching, for fine detail work, and for viewing artwork more effectively.

"Neo-white, the incandescent bulbs of pure white light, made with neodymium oxide," Kassel says "are cooler because they emit twenty percent less infrared energy."

Bill Hudson markets a variety of good health products through his Smyrna, Georgia-based company, Pure Health Concepts. Hudson offers full-spectrum indoor lighting for promoting proper bodily function. He says that light is one of the four basic elements required by the body to function correctly. The same as the other three—air, water, and nutrients—light can be nourishing or it can be polluted. Hudson provides consumers with a long-lasting (he claims 36,000 hours) full-spectrum fluorescent bulb. (To request full information and ordering procedures for all the products mentioned here, please see "Resources for More Information" on page 167.)

6.

Color Benefits From Stones and Crystals

The Orange River, a playground for the children of Hopetown, South Africa, has a water level that varies greatly. During the rainy season, the river is full from bank to bank. During the dry season, there is only a trickle of water. During the dry season in 1866, two members of the Jacobs family, a young brother and sister, found a dirty, bluish chunk of stone in the riverbed out some distance from the bank. The crystal had an unusual shape and gave off a gleaming light when held toward the Sun.

The little girl clapped her hands and said, "It will make a pretty lamp for my doll house!" She took the stone home.

The next day, Schalk van Niekerk, a neighbor, dropped in and saw the stone. He turned it over in his hand, and its glitter intrigued him. "I'd like to buy it from you."

"Nonsense!" broke in Mrs. Jacobs, the wife of a poor Boer farmer. "The children shouldn't waste their time picking up rocks. Take it for a gift."

That was the start of South Africa's growth from a frontier settlement raising only corn and cotton to the most important diamond-supplier in the world. Three years later, Van Niekerk sold the rock, which actually was a diamond, for $55,000. The diamond is now known as the "Star of South Africa" and is worth $5 million.

Diamonds, the most precious and purest in form and radiance of all the gemstones, remain emblematic of innocence and constancy. Though not actively used in medicine today, the diamond still heals by its great beauty and through its being a link with the natural forces from whose elements it was formed. These elements contain ingredients that are powerful in color healing. That the diamond has mystical virtues was attested by the ancients.

ANCIENT BELIEFS ABOUT GEMSTONES

Many people hold steadfast beliefs about certain gemstones. Some of these beliefs are part of their culture and are valuable, if for no other reason than their placebo effect. For example, an Apache medicine man is in awe of turquoise because of its magical powers. In addition to being a sort of badge of office, turquoise in an earlier era assured an Indian warrior that his arrow or bullet would speed straight to its target.

Belief in the effects of gemstones on the affairs of man was not limited to any one age or culture, but was a part of every human society, says Paul E. Desautels in his book *The Gem Kingdom*.

Each sign of the zodiac was associated in ancient times with a stone that supposedly assisted it in exerting its influence on mortals. The Christians and Jews of long ago made use of the same idea by relating certain gemstones to the Twelve Tribes of Israel and to the Twelve Apostles.

Early Jewish cabalists suggested that twelve stones, each one engraved with an anagram of the name of God, had mystical powers over the twelve angels: ruby over Malchediel, topaz over Asmodel, carbuncle over Ambriel, emerald over Muriel, sapphire over Hercel, diamond over Humatiel, jacinth over Zuriel, agate over Barbiel, amethyst over Adnachiel, beryl over Humiel, onyx over Gabriel, and jasper over Barchiel.

In addition, gemstones were related mystically to the twelve months of the year, the twelve parts of the human body, the twelve hierarchies of devils, and more. In the 1990s, we still pay economic homage to the twelve birthstones. Relating a gemstone to the birth month of the wearer gained momentum among the Jews in Poland in the eighteenth century as an outgrowth of their active interest in the significance of the original twelve gemstones in the breastplate of the Jewish high priest.

George Kunz, in *The Curious Lore of Precious Stones*, affirms that the belief in the mystical characteristics of gemstones was coupled in early times with a trust in their medicinal values. The name "jade," for example, was originally applied by Spanish conquerors in Mexico to the jade pieces they took from the Indians. The Spaniards considered the jade pieces a cure for kidney ailments. Because of this, they referred to them as *piedras de yjada*—"stones of the side"—or kidney stones. From *yjada* came our label for the stone: jade.

Some colored stones were believed to function medicinally when taken internally and others supposedly worked if applied externally to the parts of the body. Physicians in the early eighteenth century mixed fragments of gems in their medicines. To this day, amber is kept in stock by druggists in Paris for filling prescriptions. Many Chinese still use powdered pearls, coral, and other gems in medicine. Some additional ancient beliefs about the healing powers of gemstones are:

- Amber worn in beads around the neck or wrist will cure a sore throat and ague (malaria), and will prevent insanity, asthma, dropsy (ankle swelling), toothache, and deafness.
- Bloodstone prevents death from bleeding.
- Cat's-eye is a cure for croup.
- Precious coral that is swallowed will cure indigestion.
- Garnet prevents fever and dropsy.
- Jasper stops bleeding and prevents poisoning.
- Moonstone is a cure for epilepsy.
- Quartz, when powdered and mixed with water, will cure a serpent's bite.
- Ruby is a disinfectant and prevents infectious diseases.
- Sapphire cures madness and boils.
- Tourmaline, when heated, can charm away pain such as toothache.

Pliny the Elder (A.D. 23–79), in his massive, thirty-seven-volume *Historia Naturalis*, was skeptical of the curative powers assigned to gemstones. Nevertheless, he faithfully recorded the ancient beliefs, which were in tune with the superstitions of his fellow Romans. Camillus Leonardus, in his scholarly text on healing *Speculum Lapidum*, written in 1502, also assigns medici-

Signs of the Zodiac

The zodiac is an imaginary band in the heavens. It is 16 degrees in width and extends 8 degrees on either side of the ecliptic. It is divided into twelve parts or signs of 30 degrees each.

The table below gives the names and birthstones of the twelve signs of the zodiac.

Sign	Birthstone	Sign	Birthstone
Aquarius	Garnet	Leo	Onyx
Pisces	Amethyst	Virgo	Carnelian
Aries	Bloodstone	Libra	Chrysolite
Taurus	Sapphire	Scorpio	Aquamarine
Gemini	Agate	Sagittarius	Topaz
Cancer	Emerald	Capricorn	Ruby

nal powers to some gemstones. Leonardus considered malachite a powerful local anesthetic, good for pulling teeth. He felt that Sapphire was good for curing boils. And amber, he said, "naturally restrains the flux of the belly; is an efficacious remedy for all disorders of the throat. It is good against poison. If laid on the breast of a wife when she is asleep, it makes her confess all her evil deeds. It fastens teeth that are loosened, and by the smoke of it poisonous insects are driven away." However, Thomas Nicols cautioned physicians in his *Arcula Gemmea* in 1653: "Beware of the use of gems (unless you be sure they are true) in physick, by reason they are so frequently adulterated."

THE HISTORY OF GEMSTONE USAGE

The first human being who noticed a lump of fiery red opal particles imbedded in rock (perhaps in Australia), picked them out, balanced them in his hands, noticed their weight, and beat them between two rocks to shape them for personal purposes was engaged in the science and skill of gemology and gemstone application.

With certain minor exceptions, gemstones are small pieces from mineral deposits found in the earth. Their nature was not fully appreciated until the study of mineralogy was developed. Mineralogical distinctions separate gems according to their color, rarity, hardness, susceptibility to polish, and aesthetic quality. The science of gemology, concerned with investigating and establishing facts about gemstones, answers questions about where they come from, what they are made of, how they can be distinguished from one another, and how much they are worth. Gemology differs from the art of lapidary, which deals with the techniques for cutting, polishing, and generally shaping gemstones for ornamental use by themselves or in jewelry. Lapidary work has become a joint venture for the artist and the craftsman, leaning heavily on the science of gemology.

In defining the objects we are discussing, please be additionally aware that: 1. Gemstones are specially treasured minerals found in the earth; 2. Gems are objects fashioned from gemstones; and 3. Jewels are gems that have been prepared for mounting in jewelry or other objects of art. In addition, certain natural mineral samples are not gemstones but are still treasured as such because what can be cut from them has a qualifying characteristic: brilliance, beauty, color, purity, durability, rarity, or portability.

David Marcum, in his book *The Dow Jones-Irwin Guide to Fine Gems and Jewelry*, reports that over one million people in the United States spend a minimum of $2,000 each on jewelry every year. Yet of all the expensive luxuries they buy, these people know less about gems and jewelry than about any other item.

"A gemstone's origin is locked in the secrets of the formation of the cosmos," Marcum advises. "Our sun is incapable of creating, through nuclear fusion, elements that are heavier than carbon. Yet, in many stones there exist elements such as chromium, manganese, vanadium, and iron. These metals, which give emerald its rich green color, the ruby its dazzling red, and sapphire its serene blue, were not created in the sun's nuclear fusion cauldron. Rather, they were captured during the formation of our solar system, bits of galactic debris, the dead remnants of exploded stars and collapsed planetary systems."

WHAT GEMSTONES ARE

Gemstones are those minerals and other materials that possess the requisite beauty and durability to be used for personal adornment. With the exception of some organic materials, such as pearls and amber, the important gemstones are minerals, most of which are crystalline. Whenever a crystalline mineral is created in nature, its atoms form a three-dimensional pattern that is characteristic of it alone. The various patterns that atoms can form this way can be classified into six crystal systems. Since the atoms of a given mineral always assume the same pattern, a mineral always crystallizes in the same system. The properties, or characteristics, of each mineral are determined by its chemical nature and the pattern assumed by its atoms.

Again, gemstones depend for their beauty on the properties of brilliancy, dispersion (prismatic fire), color, luster, and (rarely) unusual optical effects such as the opal's play of color. Thus, a transparent mineral without body color, such as a diamond, is valued for its unsurpassed brilliancy and flashes of fire. Rubies and emeralds are cherished for their lovely colors; pearls for their warm colors, iridescent effect called "orient," and luster; and cat's-eye for its color and attractive "eye."

THE CHANGING COLORS OF GEMSTONES

Gemstones have color, which makes one of the most significant impressions on our senses when we fix our attention on any mineral, whether the mineral is used for ornamentation, technical-mechanical purposes, medical purposes, or other purposes. Still, most gem minerals do not have any color if they are chemically pure. Color is usually contributed by the selective absorption of the white light transmitted through, and reflected from, them. The usual pigmentary agents are minute amounts of metallic oxides; for example, the red of a ruby, as well as the green of an emerald, fine jade, and demantoid garnet, are each caused by the presence of a minute amount of chromium oxide. However, there are also many other causes of color in gems.

The refractive index, the ratio of the velocity of light in air to its velocity in the gem material, determines the potential brilliancy of a stone. The diamond has one of the highest refractive indexes among transparent materials. Other factors also affect the brilliancy of a faceted stone, including transparency, proportions, and polish. The angles of the crown and base facets, and the polish on a transparent gem have significant effects on its brilliancy, prismatic fire, and intensity of color. Thus, proper proportioning is a major factor in bringing out the maximum beauty from a rough mineral.

Specific gravity, or the density of the material, determines the size of a stone per carat of weight.

In addition to possessing beauty, a gem must be sufficiently durable to permit its use as an object of personal adornment. Durability depends on hardness (resistance to abrasion) and toughness (resistance to cleavage and fracture). The hardness of a mineral is measured against an arbitrary scale developed by the German mineralogist Friedrich Mohs (1773–1839), assigning to the diamond, the hardest mineral, an arbitrary hardness of 10, and to talc, the softest mineral, a hardness of 1. Mohs' hardness scale includes: diamond, 10; corundum, 9; topaz, 8; quartz, 7; feldspar, 6; apatite, 5; fluorite, 4; calcite, 3; gypsum, 2; and talc, 1. Stones rated below 7 on the scale are more subject to surface abrasion than stones rated 7 or higher.

Gem Colors From A to Z

The various wavelengths of the visible spectrum, which together compose white light, are reduced in velocity unequally when passing through a gem. Since this gives rise to an unequal refraction of the different wavelengths, flashes of vivid color emerge. This property is called dispersion, or fire. Synthetic rutile, diamond, and demantoid garnet possess strong dispersive powers.

Some gemstones have the property of resolving a single beam of light into two beams as it passes through them; this is called double refraction. In a few stones, the two beams are absorbed unequally and emerge as different colors; this is known as dichroism. The beauty of the color of gems such as ruby and sapphire is due in part to the blending of the dichroic colors.

Studies of the human response to the colors in gemstones show that the perception of hue is best in the central part of the spectrum and decreases toward either end. Thus, yellow-green, yellow, and yellow-orange as a rule appear brighter in gems than the hues that range from yellow-green to violet and from yellow-orange to red.

When observed in the decreased light of evening, the colors at either extreme of the spectrum, namely red and violet, seem to become darker in stones, while those near the center of the spectrum tend to retain their visibility. In colored gems, therefore, dark red, blue, and violet are less likely to "hold" their hues in evening illumination than yellow, orange, and yellow-green. Thus, the person contemplating buying an expensive piece of jewelry meant to be worn mainly at evening functions would certainly be wise to first test the piece under the expected lighting condition rather than under that in the jewelry store or outside.

Moreover, color hues in gemstones toward the violet end of the spectrum, the so-called "cool" colors, tend to depress the spirits, while those toward the other or "warm" end of the spectrum tend to excite. A red ruby, for instance, is stimulating to the libido.

The most attractive gemstone colors are those that are pure and rich in hue, such as red, green, blue, purple, orange, and yellow. Of these hues, the first three are the most attractive, while purple and orange are slightly less attractive. There is a substantial drop of interest in yellow. Interest also wanes in hues that become increasingly darker or lighter with changing lighting conditions or that are gradated as a norm. The least attractive are gemstones that display some shade of brown, particularly if they are quite dark. Black and white gemstones are not fetching either, although they may be in vogue for brief periods, as was jet black during the Victorian era. Colorless gems are unattractive unless, as in the case of faceted diamonds, they display good brilliance with good dispersion or "fire."

Listed in Table 6.1 are the most frequently used gemstones with their colors.

BIRTHSTONES

A birthstone is a gem assigned to a specific month of birth. The use of birthstones is recorded in the Old Testament. Aaron, the

Table 6.1. Popular Gemstones and Their Colors

Gemstone	Colors
Amber	Red-brown to yellow
Beryl	Light greenish blue, intense green, red, yellow, colorless
Chrysoberyl	Green in daylight, red in artificial light
Coral	Orange to red
Corundum	Red, blue, purple, yellow, orange, green, colorless
Diamond	Colorless, yellow, brown, light red, blue, green, violet
Feldspar	Bluish green, white, yellow, golden spangled
Garnet	Dark red, violet-red, brownish violet, yellow, brown, green
Hematite	Metallic dark gray
Jade	Green, white, violet, brown, blue, gray, black
Lapis lazuli	Dark blue with flecks of yellow pyrite
Malachite	Light and dark green bands
Opal	White, dark gray, black with vivid color flashes
Pearl	White, cream, gray, black, all with iridescent overtones
Peridot	Green
Quartz	Purple, yellow, brown, colorless
Spinel	Red, blue, violet
Spodumene	Red-violet
Topaz	Brown, yellow, blue, light red, colorless
Tourmaline	Green, red, purple
Turquoise	Light blue
Zircon	Blue, colorless, green, brown, orange, red

brother of Moses, was a high priest, and his breastplate was jeweled with twelve precious stones. These stones eventually became linked with first the twelve signs of the zodiac and then the twelve months of the year. The assignment of certain stones to particular months varied with the teachings of different peoples. Separate listings that do not coincide with each other were issued by the ancient Jews, Romans, Arabians, Poles, Russians, and Italians; Isidore Bishop of Sevil; and modern, industrialized Westerners. In modern times, the jewelry industry accepts the listing in Table 6.2.

There are many colors that you should be using to bring balance to your everyday life. Your moods change. Your job can be demanding. Your marriage may be upsetting at times. As a result, your surroundings call for different colors according to the demands of your daily activities. Your birthstone will go a long way toward directing you to what colors are right for you.

NATURAL QUARTZ CRYSTAL STONES

Sometimes referred to in ancient tradition as the "veins of the Earth," natural quartz crystals are formed from the elements silicon and water. Their natural formation features six faces and

Table 6.2. Currently Accepted Birthstones

Month	Gem
January	Garnet
February	Amethyst (transparent quartz)
March	Bloodstone or aquamarine (beryl)
April	Diamond
May	Emerald (beryl)
June	Pearl, moonstone, or alexandrite
July	Ruby (corundum)
August	Sardonyx or peridot
September	Sapphire (corundum)
October	Opal or tourmaline
November	Topaz
December	Turquoise or zircon

a point at one or both ends. A crystal with a point at one end is called "single-terminated," and a crystal with a point at both ends is called "double-terminated." Often, several crystals are joined in a cluster with a common base. A single crystal has probably broken off from a cluster.

Quartz crystals can either be colorless or come in a variety of colors. Each color has its own vibration rate, which forms an energy field around the stone. The energy field is the healing power of the crystal; a crystal with a one-inch diameter projects a field of approximately six feet. Also important for a crystal's healing power are its clarity and brilliance. The energy flows from the bottom of the crystal to its top in a definite line of power transmission and direction. As it transforms energy, it expands and contracts slightly at differing rates, depending on the rate of its color crystal vibration. This expansion and contraction (oscillation) of a crystal make it valuable for radio and television broadcasting; the oscillations create electromagnetic radio and television waves.

Crystals can be charged with energy by a few methods. They take power from sunlight, running water (ocean waves, running streams, waterfalls, and even water flowing from a sink tap), and rushing wind. They also become revved up with energy from being buried in the earth for a time, being sunk in sand at the beach, and sitting outdoors overnight in the moonlight. Before a natural quartz crystal is used for healing, it should be charged through one of these processes to gain maximum power.

Quartz crystals come in a whole family of colors. They include purple amethyst; blue quartz; rose quartz; citrine quartz, which is pale yellow, fiery orange, or light brown; green quartz; rutilated quartz, which has fine gold- or copper-colored fibers; and clear quartz, with black, blue, or green tourmaline rods within.

TECHNIQUES OF GEM CHROMOTHERAPY

Gems and crystals are used in chromotherapy for their potent effects. But some stones are more potent in their healing poten-

tial than others because of particular characteristics. The best
healing stones:

- Have the purest color.
- Are not mixed with any other colors or artifacts (called in-
  clusions).
- Are concentrated, with rays lying inside the gem.
- Reveal a true gem color when viewed through a prism. For
  example, the rays of a diamond, which seem white to the
  naked eye, are in fact indigo when seen through a prism.
  Table 6.3 gives the true ray color of some of the gemstones
  used in chromotherapy.

Gem therapy can be applied by having the individual to be
healed wear the healing stones as a necklace, ring, bracelet, or
other ornament. Gemstones can be mixed. In India, China, and
Egypt, gemstones are still burned according to ancient practice
to get ashes for use as medicine. In Indian marketplaces, the
ashes of specific gemstones are available for anyone to buy.
These ashes are known as *Bhasmas* and are used for the illnesses listed in Table 6.4.

Illnesses for Which the Whole Gemstone Is Used

Not many jewels or stones are used in a physical sense in modern Western medicine as they were in times past. In ancient

Table 6.3. The True Ray Color of
Some Gemstones

Gem	Ray
Ruby	Red
Pearl	Orange
Coral	Yellow
Emerald	Green
Moonstone	Blue
Diamond	Indigo
Sardonyx	Ultraviolet
Cat's-eye	Infrared

Table 6.4. Gemstone Ashes and the Illnesses They Treat

Gemstone Ash	Illnesses Treated
Ruby ash	Tuberculosis, colic, boils, ulcers, assorted aches and pains, liver trouble, eye problems, constipation, heart disease, fever, and emotional illness.
Pearl ash	Coughing, fever, heart palpitations, complexion blemishes, indigestion, mental illness, diabetes, frigidity, impotence, jaundice, alcoholism, and tuberculosis.
Coral ash	Liver trouble, parasites, ulcers, blood diseases, venereal disease, fever, leprosy, asthma, jaundice, urinary diseases, and obesity.
Emerald ash	Sterility, stammering, emaciation, loss of appetite, dumbness, deafness, kleptomania, digestive disorders, leukoderma (a birth deformity involving white skin patches), colic, asthma, hemorrhoids, ulcers, swelling, and debility.
Moonstone ash	Paralysis, stroke, tumors, emotional disturbance, hemorrhoids, and indigestion.
Diamond ash	Leprosy, tuberculosis, emaciation, delusion, ankle-swelling, diabetes, fistula, obesity, sterility, venereal disease, and diabetes.
Sapphire ash	Deafness, enlarged spleen, paralysis, ankle swelling, nervousness, and emotional diseases.

and medieval practices, jewels and stones retained their power to heal in the deeply mystical way that was known only to the practitioners. Gemstones heal in one way with beauty. Beauty in itself is a great source of therapy, and few are the gemstones that are not lovely to look at. Gemstones have exquisite substance, sheen, radiation, and color. Most are incorruptible, reminding man of his spiritual immortality. Many reflect and refract light, seeming thus to shine of their own accord.

The quality of the radiating light in a gemstone, akin to the mystical, awakens a sense of awe and spiritual conception in people who feel especially influenced by the aura spilling out from the stone.

Amber

Amber, glowing tawny yellow as the Sun, shading from light to dark, and having when processed a smooth, silk-like luster, is a gift to us from another healing agent—wood. It is the solidified and fossilized resin of a now-extinct species of conifer tree. It is therefore neither a stone nor a jewel, but a substance as fascinating as the glittering jewels hewn from solid rock or gathered, like the shy pearl or coral, from the ocean bed.

The main site for healing with amber is the throat. Amber treats such conditions afflicting this area as catarrh, ulcers, growths, soreness, hay fever, asthma, goiter, and respiratory diseases. It can be applied as a necklace, beads, or amulet. It can also be powdered and drunk in a mixture of honey.

Emerald

Emerald, exquisite with its rich green color and glowing radiance, is a form of beryl. It is efficacious in healing afflictions of the eyes, especially inflamed or bloodshot eyes. The stone is steeped in water for some hours, and the resulting lotion is applied to the eyes. It is also an antidote for poisons (in particular, snake bite) and a salve for wounds and sores.

Amethyst

Amethyst, a form of quartz, the mineral product of solid matter, ranges in shade from deep purple to palest violet. It protects its wearer from the excesses of alcohol. It allays insomnia, induces pleasant and healing dreams, and reduces throbbing, tension, and pain from headache. Its mystical colors induce meditation, lift the spirit, and offer spiritual wisdom.

Ruby

Ruby, the precious red stone, when applied to the skin of a person bitten by a poisonous snake is said to act as an antidote and draw out the venom. It also benefits the liver, spleen, gall bladder, and pancreas. It helps with diseases of the heart as well. It's effective against bleeding when ground into a powder and applied as a paste. It helps maintain mental health when worn constantly.

Turquoise

Turquoise, a greenish-blue jewel, is known as "the lucky stone" in Arabia. Its healing radiations are said to cure weak sight, allay inflammatory eye conditions when applied directly to the eyes, and relieve headaches. It treats conditions of the loins and chest, and reduces fever.

Moonstone

Moonstone, a variety of feldspar, is pale and watery in color, yet in certain lights, it takes on a milky opalescent blueness. In ancient days, it was called selenite, and much of its use in medicine was coupled with rites carried out with the moon as the focus. Fever, epilepsy, and mental illness are treated with moonstone.

Opal

Opal, a mineral form of soft quartz, shows many fine lines of color from small particles of air that are enclosed in innumerable tiny cracks upon its surface. It changes from blue to green, becomes faintly purple, then changes to red, and appears to be suffused with gold flecks. It clears the brain and revives the memory.

Jade

Jade, one of the loveliest of the gemstones, comes in hues varying from white to a deep, rich green. Some specimens are translucent while others are opaque. Jade is used for eye diseases, kidney complaints, poisonous snake bites, and intestinal troubles.

Pearl

Pearl, the jewel of great price, is soft and gentle in appearance, emitting no crystal radiance. It can be white or cream-colored, pink, or black. It is prised from the shell of a living creature, the oyster or freshwater mussel; this is the only "genuine" pearl. Synthetics or so-called "cultured" pearls are not thought to have the healing qualities of natural or genuine pearls. Genuine pearls are believed to have special therapeutic powers over the mind.

Diamond

Diamond, the ultimate precious stone, is made of pure carbon. Transparent in texture, it has a brilliant luster that irradiates light of peculiarly pure quality. Wine or water in which the jewel is steeped can be drunk by a patient for the treatment of gout; some ailments of the internal regions, such as gastritis; and problems of the heart and circulation.

Jet

Jet, known as black amber, is a compressed, very hard type of coal made of fossilized resin from forest trees, usually conifers, that grew long ago. It is ground to a powder and burned, and the resulting fumes are believed to repel the germs of plague, pestilence, and fever. Other ailments that benefit from the fumes of black jet are headaches, swelling in the neck, tooth-aches, and complaints of the stomach.

Topaz

Topaz, sometimes called peridot, comes in five colors—pink, black, white, green, and yellow. It is sometimes mistaken for chrysolite, which is yellowish-green in hue but lacks the deep, intense shading of true topaz. Topaz is useful for healing female illnesses, catarrh, lung conditions, nasal disorders, and throat diseases, as well as asthma, insomnia, and epilepsy.

Color has different meanings for different consumers. For instance, an older man purchasing perfume for a woman is the most likely to buy a brand in a pink bottle that resembles a gemstone. Pink appeals to men above the age of fifty-five, especially if they are purchasing a gift for a woman and particularly if the gift resembles a jewel-like bauble. In fact, the fascination with colored gems is pervasive and compelling. Although gems are not purchased as regularly as vegetables and meats, or even as frequently as automobiles in more affluent societies, there is too little known about them by the general public.

Rarity, beauty, hardness, and color (or colorlessness) make certain minerals precious. The diamond, the ruby, the sapphire, and the emerald are always classed as precious stones since they have these qualities. Pearls, however, are sometimes called precious gems because of their high value, but they are neither stone nor mineral—they are produced by oysters

As relating to color, gemstones may be transparent, like the diamond, sapphire, ruby, emerald, topaz, and garnet, and allow light to pass through them. Other stones of value may be translucent, like the opal, moonstone, and cat's-eye, permitting light to pass through them only diffusely or imperfectly. Again, stones may be more or less opaque, like the turquoise, agate, onyx, and jade, and not allow light to penetrate.

The comparative hardness of a precious stone is 8 or higher; a semi-precious stone usually has a hardness of 8 or less. Apart from their color, their hardness and amazing durability is what's notable about the most valuable of precious stones. Table 6.5 shows the hardness of a few of the leading stones, along with their specific gravity (their weight in relation to water). For example, a cubic inch of ruby weighs 4.02 times as much as a cubic inch of water. Hardness and weight are features that distinguish the most valuable gemstones from imitations. The hardness of the ruby and sapphire is surpassed only by that of the diamond. Diamond, for example, at 10, is the hardest of the gemstones, and the opal, at $5\frac{1}{2}$ to $6\frac{1}{2}$, is the softest.

Ancient records, whether those of the tomb, of painting, or of poetry, show that people have loved gems from the earliest of times and have always believed that they have strange magical powers. Gems—if you believe the marvelous stories told

Table 6.5. Hardness and Specific Gravity
              of Gemstones

Substance	Hardness	Specific Gravity
Diamond	10	3.52–3.53
Ruby	9	4.02
Sapphire	9	4.02
Spinel	8	3.6–4.0
Topaz	8	3.4–3.6
Emerald	7½–8	2.75–2.80
Agate	7	2.53–2.62
Amethyst	7	2.65–2.68
Onyx	7	2.60
Opal	5½–6½	1.90–2.30
Turquoise	6	2.60–2.83

about them—can guard against danger, foretell the future, decide the innocence or guilt of prisoners, and perform acts of healing.

The onyx exposes its wearer to lawsuits, bad dreams, and demons, but orange-red sard, when worn with the onyx, stops these evil influences.

The opal fades when worn by one who is insincere, deceitful, and impure.

The quartz, if burned, prevents storms; and when powdered and mixed with water, cures serpents' bites.

The ruby preserves its owner's house or vineyard from lightning and tempest; it also is a disinfectant that prevents infectious diseases.

The sapphire prevents despair and fire, and also cures madness and boils.

The topaz heals burns, and if thrown into boiling water, deprives the water of its heat.

The turquoise grows pale if its owner becomes ill, and loses its color at his death until placed upon a princess's finger.

The tourmaline when heated can charm away pain such as toothache or heel spurs.

The moonstone cures epilepsy.

The jasper prevents poisoning, stops bleeding, and halts overflowing water.

The iolite foretells storms by changing color.

The garnet makes its wearer agreeable, powerful, and victorious, plus it prevents fever and swelling.

The emerald helps its owner to win the favor of rulers and makes enemies peaceful. If the owner is unmarried, wearing the emerald causes him to become invisible.

The diamond casts a charm against danger, and gives hardiness and manhood to its owner.

Coral prevents blight, caterpillars, storms, and locusts, and charms against lightning, whirlwind, shipwreck, and fire. Swallowed, coral cures indigestion.

The agate prevents storms, counteracts poison, and stems the flow of blood.

Amber, worn in beads about the neck or on the wrist, cures sore throat and ague. Also, amber prevents insanity, asthma, dropsy, toothache, and deafness.

The bloodstone prevents death from hemorrhaging.

The cat's-eye warns its wearer of danger, storms, and troubles-to-come. It is a charm against witchcraft and cures the croup.

Thus, from the earliest times and among all peoples of the Earth, there have been legends, old wives' tales, myths, truisms, sentiments, and superstitions connected with gemstones. Sometimes (admittedly infrequently) in the modern era, they have been scientifically proven as facts.

7.

Color and the Non-Physical World

P articipants in research and invention, philosophy and psychology, biology and chemistry, physics and metaphysics are all uncovering different facets of the jewels of the terrestrial and the extraterrestrial, the earthly and the cosmos. During their studies, they are tracing the roots of the fundamental laws and principles governing the cosmic energy people designate as color. For too long, these color principles in nature have gone unrecognized, but finally they are coming into their own. For instance, chromatics, chromotherapy, or color therapy is no longer seen as a cult or fad that was recently invented or discovered. Throughout the ages, man has always combined color wisdom with philosophy, morality, charity, compassion, and good works. Science has now established some fundamental truths.

All things are in a state of vibratory flux. Everything is moving and working in its own area of activity. Every human is a vibrant, life-giving, and life-receiving individual. Every person feels vibrations, gives them off, and accepts them as if he were a magnet. Some people possess more of a magnetic personality than others, however. Most significant is that people exist under the vibrations of the Sun, and the Sun's activities come to people through various foods, emanations, and colors.

Color vibrations are found in all of life. They affect the color-recognizing physiologic cells of every living thing that absorbs color. For instance, if a patch is put over one eye of a chameleon, only half of the chameleon's body will change color to match the surface on which it crawls. A honey bee is attracted to a flower by the vibratory rate of the individual flower's color. A characteristic of every kind of plant and flower, these color vibratory rates are transmitted directly through the genes in the cells of that particular genus of the vegetable kingdom.

People send out vibrations in the form of hate, fear, and such other emotions as love and joy. Even odors and perfumes are vibratory forms. A body odor vibration can be an attractor, as are sexual pheromones, or it can be obnoxious, as is the penetrating smell of poor hygiene. Some women can wear a flower and have it stay fresh for several days, while other women will watch their flowers wilt in four hours or less.

Doctor Bernard Jensen of Hidden Valley Health Ranch in Escondido, California, has discovered some momentous miens of premeditation, praise, and prayer. From experiments with prayer, Doctor Jensen explains, he has learned that a plant will respond with excellent growth to praise, solicitation, and litany. However, condemnation of a plant by a group of people will bring stunted growth and death. A person with a so-called "green thumb" is likely to be the supplicating type. He probably issues silent or spoken prayers that are heard or sensed by the plants. Spiritual communion with plants is, therefore, probably the secret to having a "green thumb."

Doctor Jensen also teaches other things about vibrations, colors, and plants. A renowned natural health scientist, he has a small pink-glassed greenhouse in which he grows hothouse plants twice as fast and sturdy as in the usual clear-glass-enclosed greenhouse. He can put the same species of plants in a blue-tinted-glass hothouse and their growth will be stunted to about half the normal rate. Under pink-tinted glass, his plants seem to thrive, maturing faster and hardier. Color vibrations seem to have a stimulating or retarding effect on the plants.

Like the plants that respond to varying vibrations of color, human cells, organs, tissues, and other body parts each have their own vibrational frequency. We need to learn how to distinguish healthy vibrations from unhealthy ones. Wouldn't physicians find it advantageous to be able to tell an arthritic vibration from an osteoporotic one, or interpret the different types of chemical and vitamin deficiency vibrations?

THE RELATIONSHIP BETWEEN
SOUND, MUSIC, AND COLOR

Colors correlate to sounds. Suppose that you dropped a metal pan on the hard tile floor of your bathroom. The resulting sound would be unpleasant and jarring. Such a sound is considered noise. What color would you associate with it—a flash of red? Wouldn't you say that red is a noisy color? On the other hand, if you plucked a violin or guitar string, the resulting sound would be pleasing to your ears. Might you associate blue or green with the melody arising from the violin?

Essentially, a musical sound is smooth—consisting of uniform vibrations. A noise lacks this steadiness and regularity. The plucked string of a violin or guitar vibrates back and forth, producing compressions and rarefactions at regular and uniform intervals. A metallic pan crashing to the floor produces these compressions and rarefactions, too, but they are not uniform or regular. Gentle colors and harsh colors vibrate in a way similar to gentle and harsh sounds. They are jarring or healing, comparable to a jackhammer's staccato or a running brook's babble.

In their book *Sound Health: The Music and Sounds that Make Us Whole*, Steven Halpern, Ph.D., and Louis Savary, Ph.D., discuss the sound vibrations in music. Some musical vibrations can produce healing. Doctors Halpern and Savary write:

> To experience music fully is a holistic experience. It is in essence healthy, vital, therapeutic, and sacred. Thus holistic sound health pertains not only to a sound mind in a sound body, but also to a sound spirit. It is interesting to note that the old Anglo-Saxon word *hal* is the origin of four contemporary English words: *hale* (or healthy), *heal*, *whole*, and *holy*. Music is meant to be an experience that evokes all four meanings. It is not surprising, then, that for many people music is not only a healing force but also a call to holiness and wholeness.

Interviewed at his San Rafael, California, office, Doctor Halpern said, "There are corresponding relationships between musical tones and color tones. There are seven tones of the major musical scale and seven colors of the rainbow. Look at the lowest vibrating member of each scale, consisting of the key of C and the color red. The key of C is a natural harmonic at eight cycles per second, which is the dominant frequency of the human brain's alpha wave, plus it's the main frequency of the Earth. In fact, the eight-cycles-per-second frequency basically is the one to which all of Earth's life forms are attuned.

"If you take the octaves of 8, 16, 32, 64, 128, and 256, you arrive approximately at the key of C as we know it now. You then can relate the key of C to red, the key of D to orange, and correspondingly follow colors and notes on up the scale," Halpern continued. "If you show overly stimulated people colors while playing music based on those corresponding key notes, the listeners will come down from their excitations. They experience substituted states of relaxation and physiological balance. Their breathing becomes deeper and more regular, the hemispheres of their brains become synchronized, their pulse beats slow down, and more benefits accrue. They report feeling wonderful after drifting out of color and sound meditation.

"Such a method of sedation has come from the work in the early part of the twentieth century of Rolland Hunt, Ph.D., of Oxford, England. He has an excellent record of working with the neurotic and mentally ill using color and music in combination," said Halpern.

Color Vibrations in Music

Murdo MacDonald Bain, M. D., who was Doctor Bernard Jensen's mentor, was a Scottish army captain during World War I. He described how wounded Scottish soldiers lying on the battlefield—many of them badly hurt—would get up and march again when they heard the sound of bagpipes. Mental stimulation from the vibratory musical sounds caused them to rise and present themselves on the battlefield to the best of their ability as whole men. The bagpipe vibrations inspired and moved them.

No doubt every one of us has cried from hearing sad music and felt our spirits soar from the joy of music that touched our hearts.

In experiments performed on fish, scientists played recorded rock and roll music under water, and watched the fish turn away from the stereo speaker and hurriedly leave the vicinity of the harsh vibratory sounds. Alternately, playing the "Blue Danube Waltz" had the fish return and swim right up to the speaker. They even arrived in pairs and seemed to dance with each other!

As he described in his interview, Doctor Steven Halpern has created a system that correlates the vibratory notes of the musical scale with the vibratory rainbow colors of the spectrum. Table 7.1 presents his correlations—what I call "the sounds of color"—in a very simple chart.

Although it doesn't quite manage to do so, the Halpern system tries to confirm work done with music and color by the Greek philosopher Pythagoras (585–495 B.C.). Much of the Pythagorean philosophy is confusing because of dissension among Pythagoras' disciples and the intermixture of later speculation with the earlier doctrine. Yet some of the chief principles are very clear. Among Pythagoras' discoveries in musical theory and color concepts is that basic musical harmonies depend on very simple numerical ratios between the dimensions of the instruments (strings, pipes, disks) producing them. This discovery led Pythagoras to interpret the world as a whole through numbers. This next discovery in turn was the basis for the Pythagorean theory of numbers and the subsequent development of the science of mathematics by Greek scientists.

Table 7.1. The Sounds of Colors

Note	Color
C	Red
D	Orange
E	Yellow
F	Green
G	Blue
A	Indigo
B	Violet

Doctor Halpern explained, "Today, those of us involved in color and music therapy—often called 'New Age' but recognized on another level as actually being 'ancient age'—accept Pythagoras as one of the ideological patron saints of New Age. Most often Pythagoras is recognized by New Age proponents as a master musician, educator, healer, philosopher, and mathematician. He used music and color as combined healing arts. Personally, I feel very much tapped into that tradition of the master."

Author Dorothy Retallack, writing in *The Sound of Music and Plants*, discusses the sounds of color, too, according to Pythagoras' theory. But Retallack also fails to fully tie into Pythagoras' concepts. For this reason, Halpern's, Retallack's, and Pythagoras' data do not entirely agree. For example, while Halpern states that the key of C is red, Retallack says the key of C is yellow-green. Which of them agrees with Pythagoras? Pythagorean history does not tell us.

Retallack writes:

Pythagoras, upon listening to the musical scale, realized that the scale could be expressed by numerical ratios, and tones thought to be opposite were actually complementary. Concluding that high and low pitch could be brought together harmoniously, then all seeming opposites might also have a harmonious relationship. This was a breakthrough in understanding the secrets of the cosmos and life. Plato said that Pythagoras made music and astronomy sister sciences. . . .

When the magical power of sound and color are rediscovered and directed to specific purposes, there will be energies of a higher dimension transcending those unleashed by the atom today.

As did Halpern, Retallack correlates the notes of the C major scale with their corresponding vibrational colors, but she goes on to give the Pythagorean meanings of the notes and the esoteric meanings of the colors. Table 7.2 presents Retallack's chart.

Retallack concludes, "The therapeutic value of both color and music has long been recognized, but it remains to be seen

Table 7.2. The Musical Notes and Their Vibrational Colors and Meanings

Musical Note	Color	Vibrations Per Second	Pythagorean Note Meaning	Esoteric Color Meaning
A	Red Orange	213	Absolute, Creative Force, The One— Undifferentiated	Either Health or Destruction
B	Yellow	240	Descending into dense form Animal & plant level of manifestation	Understanding Unity Power of will Service
C	Yellow-Green	256	Purification of that form, the turning point out of the animal form into the divine	Love Chastity
D	Green-Blue	288	Vitality given to human forms	Discriminating Renewal of spiritual forces
E	Blue-Violet	320	Harmony—bring together higher & lower natures in peace, Healing	Healing Cleansing
F	Violet	341	Formation, Tone of Nature Perfection visualized	Awaken spiritual power
G	Deep Red	384	Gratitude, Positive Force Lifting	Releases forces of spiritual illumination
A	Red Orange	427	One with Nirvana Consciously raising the self from imprisonment in animal instincts	Development of etheric vehicle

SOURCE: Retallack, Dorothy. *The Sound of Music and Plants* (Marina Del Rey, CA: DeVorss & Company, 1973).

whether the theories that have been advanced can find practical application in modern healing practices."

Sound Compared to Color

The simplest sound consists of a series of waves that moves through the air with a velocity of just over 1,000 feet per second. Sound waves are different from waves traveling on the surface of water. Sound waves have alternate zones of compression and rarefaction while water waves have alternate crests and troughs. But they are each still a true wave series in the sense that they repeat both in space and in time.

According to the Pythagorean chart furnished by Dorothy Retallack, the musical note of middle C gives out as its fundamental tone a series of regularly spaced air waves that strike the ear 256 times per second (on the scientific pitch).

The average person can hear down to about 8 vibrations a second, which is what human ears can pick up at the low-frequency end of the scale. He can hear up to 3,200 vibrations in a second at the high-frequency end. Beyond this range are other frequencies, but no person can hear them.

Likewise, vibrations of colors occupy the visible range of light frequencies. Each color has its own frequency, and humans can see 8 million different frequencies or gradations of color.

Smells also vibrate. Perfume has its own vibration. Every odor occupies its own frequency. The great perfumist Matchebelli could distinguish and name 500 different perfume scents with his olfactory nerves. The olfactories are 27,000 nerves located in the nasal passages that send messages to the olfactory center of the brain. Olfactory nerve messages are sent by vibration.

When sound frequencies are related to colored flowers and vegetables, such as the sunflower or yellow corn, an interesting phenomenon takes place. First, the "face" of a sunflower follows the Sun as it crosses the sky during the day. This is, of course, the main reason the flower was named "sunflower." Amazingly, however, if noisy rock and roll music is played from the same direction the Sun is in, the sunflower will turn away. It will not follow the Sun. But substitute classical or other reposeful music, and the sunflower will readily turn back and face the Sun.

Second, experiments with yellow corn performed by the School of Agriculture of Iowa University show that certain music can increase the husk yield of yellow corn. The yellow color must be a factor because it doesn't work with white corn.

Some vibrations can be destructive. For instance, 60 percent of the disc jockeys who work full-time with rock and roll music are partially deaf from the loud noises they send out over the airwaves. Moreover, auditory measurements taken of the graduating students at the University of California uncovered that 30 percent of the students were hearing-impaired from the noisy music they had enjoyed during their college years.

Matter in motion produces vibration, and vibration alters the structure of other matter by changing its vibration and the shape of the matter it then acts upon. Thus, the Earth is saturated with vibrational effects, from cosmic radiation to microwave ovens to country music to grinding engines to radar to television satellites to kaleidoscopic colors and more. Violent turbulence, gentle flows, interpenetrating streams of movement—all from vibrations—produce thousands of unusual earthly patterns. These affect the mind and the body of man to produce illness or wellness, depending on the quality and quantity of the stressors.

The Sound and Color of the Soul

Visiting the city of Dunedin, a Scottish settlement on the South Island of New Zealand where plaids with their multicolors are habitually worn, Doctor Bernard Jensen witnessed bagpipes being played melodiously by the residents. One of the renditions he heard was "Amazing Grace," an important hymn because of its healing qualities. These New Zealanders of Scottish descent claim that more healings have been accomplished with "Amazing Grace" than with any other piece of music. The souls of the healed people must respond to what they hear.

As mentioned earlier, color and sound are alike in that they both consist of a series of waves (vibrations) in the air. As sound, the waves strike the eardrum and make it vibrate. As color, they strike the retina and make the eye react. Sound vibrations act through a complex mechanism of bone and cartilage, stimulating impulses in the fibers of the auditory nerve. When the nerve impulses reach the brain, the listener gets the sensation of noise, speech, or music. With the eye, image information is transferred to the brain by way of the retina through the optic nerve. That is, light and color that fall on the retina are not interpreted by the retina, but are sent along to the visual cortex of the brain in the rear of the head. Then the interpretation is made. The principle on which the eye operates is essentially the same as that of a camera. (The camera is the only manmade mechanism modeled on a human sense organ.)

If the retina views a horrible scene, the pupil of the eye will contract 50 percent. A beautiful and pleasant scene will cause a 50 percent dilation. Why is unknown. Medical science is still seeking an answer to the many questions: Where and why does the pupil's contraction begin? What causes it? Can nerve or endocrine chemicals see? Can chemicals decide whether something is horrible or beautiful, and then cause a corresponding change in the size of the eye's pupil?

From his broad range of knowledge about the physiological effects of color, Doctor Jensen has attempted to answer these questions. He suggests that the body is a medium for the experiences needed or desired by the spiritual part of a human being, which is the portion responsible for thinking and willing, and hence determining all behavior. This "soul" is not chemical in nature, but it does feed on vibrations just as the body feeds on fruits, vegetables, nuts, and seeds. All of us are created from chemical elements, but man is much more than a network of complex chemical molecules. As opposed to plants and other animals, man includes this spiritual element.

The Bible says: *And the Lord God formed man of the dust of the ground, and breathed into his nostrils the breath of life; and man became a living soul.*

Certain philosophers, such as Descartes, Spinoza, Leibnitz, Locke, and the Occasionalists, considered the soul as essentially substance, finished once and for all at the creation of the universe. Locke said the soul is the substratum of ideas, a blank tablet on which the ideas are impressed. Self-consciousness exists, he stated, but beyond this, Locke did not characterize it.

Others put forth that the soul is consciousness in the embodiment of a form or structure or relation in the stream of consciousness itself. It has color as manifested by the body's aura.

THE AURAL COLORS AROUND US

From the stained glass of ancient church windows and religious paintings to modern research involving magnetic fields, radar scopes, wave signals from satellites, and other waves from invisible stars in outer space, we are cognizant of halos of light all around us. People also radiate halos. Their halos have colors, shades of which are diagnostic to those who can see them. They project the power of personality, extent of spirituality, intensity of feeling, quality of healing, strength of will, and resolution of purpose of the individual.

The disciplines of metaphysics and parapsychology teach that there is mankind the human body and mankind the spiritual being. Metaphysics is a branch of philosophy that deals with the first principles of being and knowledge, and with the essential nature of reality. Parapsychology is the detailed investigation of psychic phenomena, such as extrasensory perception and telepathy.

Distinctly different from mankind the human body, mankind the spiritual being—considered by metaphysicians to be represented by a light halo of the spirit—is called *the aura.*

The aura is an invisible suit of colors that each of us wears. The colors remain unseen only by those who refuse to look for the higher consciousness of mankind. But the aura is there, declare the metaphysicians, and is a permanent "other self." It surrounds the physical body as a source of heat conservation and protection that decreases and increases as the environment changes. It leaves behind pictures of itself and can be photographed without the use of a camera. Our human aural colors derive from the Earth's magnetism and its north-south polarity.

The Earth's Magnetic Current

North of the equator, the north rail of an east-west train track invariably wears down first. South of the equator, the south rail always wears out first.

Above the equator, an oil well that blows, or comes in, always blows itself toward the North Pole. It blows to the South Pole when below the equator.

Closer to the North Pole, wisteria vines grow around to the right. But closer to the South Pole, they grow around to the left.

If you turn on a water faucet in New York City, the water in the sink will always swirl around to the right before it goes down the drain. In the Australian city of Brisbane, the water will swirl around to the left. These swirling waters are affected by the pole to which they are closer.

These phenomena are not the result of occult beliefs or psychic works. They are actual physical forces related to the powerful vibrations of the magnetic waves or frequencies that are as real as gravity and wind.

Because the Earth has a constantly moving magnetic stream, a captain can navigate his ship in unknown waters with the certainty that he will reach his destination. The Earth's magnetic lines of force extend outward from one magnetic pole, level off over the geomagnetic equator, and then bend downward to converge at the opposite magnetic pole.

The same as the Earth, the human body also has a magnetic field, with polarity existing between the soles of the feet and the top of the head. In fact, everyone requires the essential energies of the Earth's currents and electronic fields. Applying them facilitates the various personal metabolic communications, such as between the cells, to the immune system, from the hormonal messengers, as nerve impulses, and as exchanges of ionization in the bloodstream and tissue fluids. Personal magnets surround the body as well in the form of the variably colored halo—the aura. This aural structure is an atmosphere emanating from the individual. It is a person's astral body, composed of three separate layers—an etheric body, a soul body, and a spirit body—all of which are created from ascending vibratory rates. The spirit body is the highest.

The Aural Structure

Our senses and feelings come from electrons and the minute electrical impulses they send through our nervous system. An electron is a charged particle with an electrical field that extends in every direction, theoretically for an infinite distance. The vibrating electrons inside our body make electromagnetic waves; and unless we do something to shield the components, those waves move off in all directions like ripples in water. When the waves hit another electrical circuit that generally responds to the same frequency, they can activate that circuit. The minute electrical impulses are then transported to the brain, where they are reconverted into signals, messages, images, and more. The brain cells feed back any suitable response.

Surpluses of these electrical nerve impulses are fed to the surface of the skin. The skin thus also becomes charged with the personal feelings we know as our emotions. Blushing is a physical example of such an emotional charge. These electrical surpluses are the foundation for the aural structure and are manifested as six different colors.

Along with this, the brain also generates minute amounts of electricity for its intercommunication areas, which are additionally charged with thought energies. These electrical energies fill places around the body with thought waves or mental vibrations. These, too, integrate themselves as part of the aura.

Then we have a fourth-dimensional domain, the extrasensory extension of our "other self." This is an invisible part, seen only by those individuals who possess a "higher" awareness, such as the now-deceased psychics Edgar Cayce and Edith Worrell.

Your halo colors encircle your body in an oval shape and represent your higher state of being. They are the part of you that is the closest to the Absolute Eternal Being, which some people refer to as God.

The outermost layer of your aural being is the soul or spiritual side. Its aura is colored deep blue to violet. The soul forms a sort of body attached to the spirit and acts as an intermediary with the more superficial dimensions. It was formed first—before the mind, the emotions, and the body substance.

Shaped in the third-dimensional sphere of reality, the aura is divided into three parts: the head, the body, and the organs of mobility (the lower limbs or, if a person walks on his hands, the upper limbs). Each aural representation can act separately and have different colors. When the individual is in homeostasis, his aura is expanded and vibrant with color. When he is in distress—such as ill, traumatized, cold, fearful, or anxious—the six-fold colors of his aura contract close to his body and hardly glow at all. The aura of wellness shines bright and clear while the aura of illness appears turgid or dark brown. A body that is overworked, fatigued, or drained of energy seems sadly gray and inert. The natural color of the aura surrounding a body structure is usually whitish gray.

As mentioned, the aura of a happy and healthy fully evolved adult person is divided into six vivid colors. Closest to the body is the neutral tone of white. Next comes glowing red, followed by bright yellow, green, and blue. Violet or indigo is the outermost layer. The colors come from the light within you that arises from a universal radiance fueled by your diet, the positive image you project to others, the amount of rest you get, exercise that "unstresses" your physiology, and other components of a wholistic lifestyle. If you live a distressed existence, your aura will be shrunken and exceedingly difficult to identify. Your aural colors can be heightened or shaded, or otherwise affected, by the techniques of chromotherapy.

Visualizing the Aura With Kirlian Photography

Kirlian photography (radiation-field photography) is a means of taking pictures of the nonmaterial world without a camera. It provides a way of viewing the unseen patterns of energy and force fields that probably permeate all substances. It offers mankind a tool with which to view art, religion, and science. It can serve as a medical diagnostic instrument, too. The Kirlian effect is useful for recording energy balances and harmonies in all forms of life.

At Krasnodar in Southern Russia near the Black Sea in 1939, a physicist named Semyon Kirlian produced photographs showing plant leaves and human hands emitting strange lights. The industrialized Western countries heard nothing about this discovery until 1970 when Lynn Schroeder and Sheilah Ostrander published their book *Psychic Discoveries Behind the Iron Curtain*. In the book, they wrote about Kirlian's discovery. Kirlian claimed that he made photographs of energy or "radiation

The Rainbow Bridge

"Suppose you went to bed tonight and you dreamt you were a rainbow. Wouldn't that be a nice dream? But if you wake up in the morning and you say, 'Last night I dreamt I was a rainbow,' now can you really say whether you're a man dreaming that you're a rainbow or whether you're a rainbow dreaming that you're a man? When you wake up you're just another ocean—you're a rainbow dreaming that you are a man—an awakened man. How do you validate the fact that you're not a rainbow dreaming that you're a man?"

These significant questions were asked during a lecture delivered November 14, 1976, at the University of the Trees in Boulder Creek, California, by Doctor Christopher Hills, an internationally renowned Master of Consciousness and a true Yogi of the New Age. I visited Doctor Hills seven years after that lecture to discuss his concepts of the spiritual truths of the aura.

Doctor Hills gave me a gift, Nuclear Evolution: Discovery of the Rainbow Body, *the second edition of a book he had written. In the book, Doctor Hills describes the Rainbow Bridge, an ancient symbol for the "Seven Worlds of Being" that each individual soul must eventually cross. In the allegory, the symbolic myth of Asgard, Asgard is the home of the Norwegian gods and has an armed sentinel named Heimdal who stands on the bridge of the seven rainbow colors that connects Earth to heaven. Heimdal is the symbol for the ego or self-sense. The gods must pass over the rainbow bridge on their way to Asgard. Additionally, dying Norse heroes are carried by the Valkyrie maidens over the rainbow bridge (also representing the seven levels of consciousness) to Valhalla, which is the state of peace and bliss that exists in Asgard.*

> *Interpreting the Norsemen's symbolism, Doctor Hills writes:*
>
> > *Their knowledge of death and the structure of consciousness was far superior to ours since they knew what we do not, that the soul of man lives on in seven different worlds of being which transcend the physical senses. Yet in our own blindness we believe them to be ignorant because we do not understand their symbolic language.*

fields" with a special process he had developed but refused to reveal. His secrecy disturbed the worldwide scientific community, but it did not detract from the importance of his photographic effects.

However, scientists did not know how to evaluate what seemed to be a substantiation of the aura or holy halo that Catholicism and other religions claimed for themselves. But parapsychologists, who had declared that they were able to see auras with the naked eye, took to Kirlian photography like ducks to water. They pointed to it as tangible proof that the aura exists.

The Kirlian photographic effect uses no lens, no camera, no sunlight, no photo floodlight, no flashbulb—in fact, no light at all. It's strictly an energy picture. The process takes place as the result of a spark discharging and allowing a whole complex of radiations to emit from the object being photographed on a film emulsion. In simple terms, the equipment consists of a metal plate and a generator or oscillator that produces a high-voltage field of variable pulse and frequency. Film is put in contact with the plate, and the object to be photographed is placed directly on the film. It is the aura of the photographed object that's eventually seen.

Depending upon the type of film used—instant color film, 35-millimeter black and white film, or something else with an emulsion that records images—different colors or shadings appear in a brilliant corona surrounding the object. The colors and depth of a person's corona may provide clues to his physical and emotional condition. Kirlian's wife, Valentina, discovered that pain produces unusually vivid colors when she took a picture of her leg after tripping and wrenching it. The stronger the pain, the Kirlians found, the brighter the corona colors. As the pain lessens, the colors soften to pastels.

Current researchers in Kirlian photography have noted that the aura of anxiety turns blue and yellow, then flares to a murky red. The corona changes in intensity, configuration, and color when an individual's mood or health changes. As with handwriting analysis, recognized changes in the aura of a person might warn of an impending illness in advance of any clinical symptoms. Kirlian suspected this years back when a photograph of his hand showed a blurred, chaotic energy pattern shortly before he became gravely ill with recurring cardiovascular disease. Moreover, other Kirlian photography enthusiasts have performed experiments with leaves showing a corona disturbance just before signs of pathology became visible in the plant.

The aura emanating from man has been described by yogi Ramacharaka in his book *Fourteen Lessons in Yogi Philosophy* as one or more of the seven principles of man. He lists these principles as:

1. the physical body.
2. the astral body.
3. the prana or vital force.
4. the instinctive mind.
5. the intellect.
6. the spiritual mind.
7. the spirit.

Most people cannot actually view the aura with their naked eye, but some can instinctively sense it. It's the individual's aura that is being described when you say: "He is a cold fish!" or "She has a magnetic personality!" or "He gives off bad vibes!" or "She is warm and friendly!" or "He gives me the creeps!" or "What a radiant smile on that man!"

In a perfectly marvelous book, *The Living Aura: Radiation Field Photography and the Kirlian Effect*, written by Kendall Johnson, the author tells how pictures of Earth made from the moon by the National Aeronautical and Space Administration (NASA) show it surrounded with a bluish luminescence. One of the first pictures of man on the Moon released by NASA shows an astronaut walking in his space suit surrounded by a cloud of blue light. The Earth and the astronaut both appear to display an aura.

Aural Radiations That Surround Us

Cosmic rays, light rays, X-rays, microwave rays, broadcasting rays from radio and television waves, short-wave rays, heat rays, sound rays, and a variety of additional radiations are bombarding us all of the time. When we eat irradiated food or inhale the smoke of cigarettes that give off radiation, we are exposing our insides to this radiation. Indeed, our physical body also radiates and affects other people within its range. Brain waves, the heartbeat, and other aspects of the soma and psyche are sending signals that can be picked up at a small distance and monitored by sensitive instruments. Radiation from our physical aura can be recorded as well.

A Supersensonic kundalini device, for instance, detects your aura color and determines which of forty-four natural elements is predominant in your physical body. Inside the unit is a whole octave oscillator tunable from 200 to 400 cycles per second. This oscillator functions as a physical exciting stimulus while the harmonics of the radio-magnetic field of the horizontal wave-field of the human emotional body are tuned by a magnetic dial at the center of a Turenne disk. The "thought fields" of the vertical wave-field are patterned by an array of prefixed de la Warr dial sets. These dials are permanently tuned at the rate for higher creative intelligence in the east-west wave-field. The Supersensonic kundalini device was designed by Doctor Christopher Hills of Boulder Creek, California, and was custom-made to his specifications by George de la Warr of Oxford, England, in 1960. Research by Doctor Hills has proven that nonelectronic equipment can also be used to produce the psychophysical effect of the aura with the radiative stimulator of the Supersensonic.

In his book on the aura, Kendall Johnson comments on the aura as it is sensed by yogis. He says that in the philosophical tracts of yoga, the physical aura is recorded as being colorless to slightly bluish-white. It contains fine bristles or lines extending out from the body. When a person is healthy, these emanating lines are still and bristly. If a person is ill, the lines show up as disarranged, knotted, limp, and chaotic. Yogi Ramacharaka attributes this difference in appearance to the degree to which the body is energized by the current of prana.

Johnson asks:

> Could it be that when dogs and other animals pick up the scents of other animals they are sensing phenomena relating to the physical aura?
>
> What is it that some artists throughout man's history have included in their portraits of certain great spiritual leaders? Are they representing on canvas something that they sensed? Do they see a light around Christ, a halo around Buddha? What is the mystic glow surrounding the infant Christ and the saints?
>
> What is it that we attribute to certain personalities as charisma?

The Aura of the Healer

Most people can see another person's aura in blue if they look through cobalt-blue glasses. Psychic healers visualize auras without any visual aids and see them in multiple living colors. The famed Dutch psychic Gerard Croiset sees "dark spots" in the aura of a sick person near the site of the disease. Often when he is "tuned in" to a patient, he also sees the *chakras*—the energy centers of the body that Eastern mystics describe. As he heals with energy from his hands, Croiset claims to observe the colors of the aura changing. "I can see pain leaving the body," he says.

Another healer, Reverend Mildred Strano, formerly of Los Angeles, sees three colorful layers in the aura. She describes the layer closest to the body as showing different colors at different points—red near the heart, yellow with pink near the spleen, and other colors in other locations.

The second layer of aura she visualizes is a beautiful, delicate yellow color when the patient's mind is healthy, but "wobbly like Jello" when the patient has a mental disorder.

The outer layer of aura that Reverend Strano sees is the astral or desire body, which shows up as a solid color and should be a healthy ruby red or rose. An excess of lust lurking in an individual is signaled by a liver-red astral body. Reverend Strano told Helen Kruger, the author of *Other Healers, Other Cures*, "I can always tell a prostitute walking down the street because there's an ugly deep red color, very exaggerated around the hips."

Kruger told of psychiatrist John Pierrakos, M. D., who does not claim to be a psychic healer but who regularly sees auras surrounding the people he meets. Kruger writes:

> Dr. Pierrakos sees three auric layers which he defines as an interstate, or bridge, between energy and matter. The first layer is about one-half inch deep and is like a void, which shows whatever color is in the background. Then comes a blue envelope-like layer which can turn red when the person is angry, or deeper blue, gray, or yellow when there is illness. Finally comes a light blue encircling haze that is also related to health. Most significant, according to Dr. Pierrakos, is that the aura is smooth and continuous in a healthy person but interrupted in one who is ill mentally or physically.

Kirlian photographs were made by Russian scientists of a healer's thumb. When the healer was photographed in his normal state, not in a healing attitude, there were corona-like flares leaping out of his thumb with long tongues of luminescence and flame. The healer's finger was literally alive with a sort of cold fire. When the healer was asked to tune in to a patient and do some healing, the Kirlian photograph taken immediately afterward showed a great reduction in the flaring, a minimization of the discharges emanating from the thumb, and a quite different condition compared with the healer's normal state.

In the United States, Kendall Johnson duplicated the Russian healer experiment with similar results. Using Kirlian photography, Johnson first made energy images of an American healer's finger pads before the healer engaged in a healing operation on one dozen kidney-impaired patients who periodically required kidney dialysis to stay alive. Johnson made aura images of the healer's fingers in color and in black and white. Next he made energy images of the patients' finger pads prior to the healing experience. Then the healer performed his ministrations, and Johnson made energy images of the healer's finger pads and of all the patients' finger pads after the experience.

The Kirlian researcher also enlisted the help of ordinary individuals as healer controls to check for placebo effects. The controls play-acted at a healing session, pretending to the real patients to be healers. The kidney-impaired persons did not know the difference.

Before the healing session, the aura of the true healer displayed clear, even, blue coronas on the color film. The coronas were strong and flaring. After the healing experience, the healer's fingerprints became weak and the coronas became interrupted; his colored Kirlian finger-imprint image tended to produce a red blotch.

The patients' finger coronas also displayed changes after the healing session. Before the session, they were in a stage of arousal, showing thin coronas, broken coronas, and vague blotches. After the healing, they showed large, clear, and flaring coronas and clear fingerprints as if they had absorbed aura from the healer.

There was little or no change in the finger images of the fake healers, and the subjects showed hardly any change after being exposed to them.

In remarkable Kirlian photographs reproduced in his book, Johnson shows the before and after pictures of his experiment with the healer. He does not declare that the patients were able to discard kidney dialysis after the healing session, but he does write, "Some interesting things did happen with these kidney patients. There were reports of headaches that were cleared up, reports of dizziness that went away, reports of improvements in blood chemistry, subjective reports of feeling better, and so on. Whether or not we can attribute these improvements to the healing session, we do not know, but it did occur."

HOW TO USE A PENDULUM TO
DETERMINE YOUR HEALING COLOR

In employing chromotherapy for healing purposes, a pendulum can be put into service as a diagnostic instrument to learn which colors are required. *Webster's Ninth New Collegiate Dictionary* defines a pendulum as "a body suspended from a fixed point so as to swing freely to and fro under the action of gravity and commonly used to regulate movements (as of clockwork).* Yes, a pendulum is this, but it is much more as well.

A pendulum is a divination or dowsing device that measures a person's inner and outer energies and force fields. It consists of a weight suspended from a string, which is held between your thumb and index finger. The weight swings to and fro, and its movements indicate positive and negative responses to your questions. The ultimate consequences and benefits of the pendulum's use are incalculable. It eliminates uncertainty in decision-making and problem-solving. Pendulum power knows no boundaries and can only increase your quality of living by offering you the answers that you need.

Using crayons or paints in the seven rainbow colors, write the name of the person to be healed seven times, once with each color. Write the color used beside each name. The list should look like the example in Table 7.3.

Now tell your subconscious that you are looking for the person's basic, or resonant, color. Then hold the pendulum

Table 7.3. Color List for Use With Pendulum

Person's name—RED
Person's name—ORANGE
Person's name—YELLOW
Person's name—GREEN
Person's name—BLUE
Person's name—INDIGO
Person's name—VIOLET

---

*Reprinted by permission. From *Webster's Ninth New Collegiate Dictionary* © 1990 by Merriam-Webster Inc., publisher of the Merriam-Webster® dictionaries.

over each name and color on the list one by one. The resonant color will be the one that produces the strongest and smoothest swing. (To learn what each color does therapeutically or means psychologically, read Chapter Five. To learn the significance of your personal reaction to a color, read Chapter Three.)

Having determined the resonant color—healing color—you should then have the individual being healed wear as much of that color as possible, moderated by good taste.

There are also other ways to use your healing color. For example, whenever fatigue hits and you have no opportunity to rest, hold some velvet ribbons of your resonant color and stare at them. This will tend to reduce your tiredness. Or, paint your bedroom in your healing color so that you are bathed in its rays and can heal while you sleep.

The pendulum is also useful for learning about your color deficiencies. Your aura, of course, is composed of all the colors of the spectrum in different proportions. The astral body maintains a delicate color balance, but when this balance is disturbed for a prolonged period, illness may result. If you feel fatigued, jittery, depressed, moody, irritable, allergic, or some other sense of inequality in homeostasis, you should check yourself for color deficiencies (in addition to nutrient deficiencies). Your aim should be to restore to your aura the colors that are reduced or missing.

Make a name and color chart as above. Then hold your pendulum over each color one by one and ask either aloud or strongly in your mind: "Am I deficient in (the color)?" The pendulum may swing positively and smoothly over one or several colors, depending on the extent of the reaction you are having to an emotional upheaval, actual illness, injury, or other distress. Whichever colors you are lacking should be restored to your aura through color therapy.

COLOR AS VIBRATORY FOOD

As quoted in the Preface, color acts as vibratory food, an external force that makes you feel good inside. It brings you into a world of beauty and upliftment—one of change. Delving into color transports you into a state of consciousness that possibly

you've never known existed. It's an environment of harmonizing effects arising from uniformity of vibrations.

The great chromotherapists of the past and present, such as
Doctor Max Luscher, Isidore Friedman, Rudolph Steiner,
George de la Warr, Doctor Bernard Jensen, and Doctor Christopher Hills, had much to say about light and color vibrations
and their nourishing effects on the body, mind, and spirit. For
instance, Doctor Hills says:

> Whenever we absorb light or radiation from the cosmic
> radiance we are in effect taking into our body the vibrat-
> ing energy caused by the activity of atoms oscillating at
> tremendous intensities in the heat of supernovas and
> stars like our sun. We do not feel this energy con-
> sciously or even acknowledge it as the source of our
> consciousness. The reason we do not experience this ra-
> diant cosmic light is because it is no different from our
> nux, our inner core of radiance. Being one and the same
> stuff it cannot tell any difference between itself and the
> cosmic background radiation which is the ground of all
> created forms. The objects we sense, the trees and stars
> and those crystals which make up our cells, are all con-
> centrations of this energy. They are held together by
> proticity [the positive form of electricity inside the nu-
> cleus of atoms] which attracts this radiating lumen and
> crystallises it into matter. All matter is crystallised en-
> ergy—crystallised light. Lumen crystallises into lux [core
> of the human soul manifested as light energy] like liq-
> uid water crystallises into solid ice through the with-
> drawal or absorption of its heat. Add some radiance
> (heat) or lumen from the light of the sun and the ice
> turns back into a liquid. Thus lux (inner light) turns
> back into lumen (pure radiant consciousness of the
> heart of the nux) by this absorption of radiant light from
> the stars. This cosmic process is going on in everything
> and not only in human bodies, human minds, and hu-
> man imaginations. The sun absorbs light from other
> more powerful suns which activate its vibrating atoms
> intensely. If it did not absorb this cosmic radiation light
> (lumen) from other stars, it would eventually slow

down its intense internal activity (its lux) and would crystallise from a gas into a liquid and thence into the crystal elements as a solid.*

Admittedly, it is difficult to accept that everything on Earth exists in the form of vibrations and that life forms or objects move from one vibration to another. The vibratory colors can be therapeutic or destructive, such as red in the different circumstances under which it is usually employed. For instance, a red flag waved in front of a bull will excite the animal into charging. In traffic, red stop signs are safety features for automobile drivers. Long underwear made of red flannel keeps you warm in winter. In the laboratory, fruit flies will breed rapidly in a red box, but will not breed at all in a blue box.

Some doctors use the color red as an arterial stimulant. Researchers at the University of Texas have discovered that athletes who concentrate on red coloring before participating in a sporting event experience increases in their muscle strength. Red can bring a flush to the head in the form of blushing.

Moreover, different colored foods have various effects on the body. Ingesting a red herb, such as cayenne pepper, brings on a feeling of heat and will actually increase body temperature. Most natural laxatives, such as senna, castor oil, peaches, apricots, figs, and fig seeds, are yellow. Yellow herbs, flowers, and seeds, and many yellow and orange squashes, such as the yellow crooked-neck squash and the wild yam, are cathartic-like in their effect when eaten. The yellow banana squash is wonderful for normalizing the digestive system because it is a slight but steady laxative.

So, you think as you see, and see what you think. When you live with a lack of color and beauty, you survive in misery, perpetually existing with hate, tension, and blackness. Such negative vibrations can be deadly. Indeed, black fear felt by an individual involves a distinct vibration that is smelled by animals and sensed by humans.

Alternatively, purple is positive—the royal color that presents itself near the end of the food-harvesting season. Pur-

---

*Reprinted with permission from Doctor Christopher Hills, University of the Trees Press, Boulder Creek, California.

ple grapes arrive in the fall. Red strawberries come in the spring. Consuming a salad that is a rainbow of colors is the best nutrition you can give your body. All of us should consume a colorful plate of vegetables at each meal, including a salad of rainbow colors. This is a means of gathering in the rainbow of vibratory foods. But remember, chefs don't cook well in a blue kitchen. Instead, yellow brings joy to food, and a chef performs more creatively in a yellow kitchen. Even green is better than blue for cooking. To work amidst shades of green allows for rejuvenation. Chlorophyll, the rejuvenator of plant life, is deep green.

But backward and retarded children seem to learn faster in rooms painted yellow.

In mental institutions, color and music are today becoming a necessary part of therapy because of their beneficial vibratory effects. Music, light, and color are more effective than psychoanalysis in reaching the emotionally disturbed. The works of John Ott on radiation, light, and color have proven their value for health.

Facing the negative reality of how color concepts are used, however, there are many aspects of mankind's explorations that are ignored, neglected, or discarded by authorities occupying the seats of power in scientific, social, medical, political, and other Establishments that could be administered for the healing of us all. Color is one of these neglected items. I anticipate that this book will cause some heavy thinking on the subject so as to transform the neglect of color in psychology, marketing, healing (chromotherapy), and spirituality into sustained attention and routine use.

Still, I wish to end on an upbeat note and put forth positive color concepts. My recommendation is that you realize you are part of the hologram of life, surrounded by an aura or energy field that radiates distinct color and vibration. The aura fingerprints your soul and reflects your goodness, wellness, mental stability, maturity, emotional/inner turmoil, or peaceful fulfillment. More of each of these qualities—peace, wellness, stability, maturity, and fulfillment—may become your ever-present precious possession by the application of color's power in your daily living.

In myriad instances, of course, society already uses the power of color for its welfare. In medicine, for instance, blue light helps in the recovery of babies from too much bilirubin, which causes jaundice.

In politics, the signifying colors of a nation's flag symbolize struggles, conquests, principles, patriotism, and pride.

In entertainment—as in card-playing—green baize on the tabletop is proven to create harmony between gamblers. Research by the Institute of Human Evolution showed that red baize irritated competitors in poker, pinochle, and other card games who quarreled and interrupted the games in the amount of 31 percent. Black on the tabletop caused the players to disrupt the game 27 percent of the time. Green, hardly at all.

In bedroom furnishings such as bedsheets, blankets, and furniture, red is totally unsuitable because of its stimulative effect on the human psyche. It causes nervousness and restlessness. You would have a difficult time falling asleep and feeling rested in a red-furnished bedroom. Brown is acceptable; green is better; blue is best for your sleeping room. More often than not, decorators suggest those calmative colors.

In transportation, the interior of a passenger airliner often is decorated with the combined shades of green and violet to reduce tension and produce relaxation among the patrons.

In stockbreeding, those who raise poultry frequently use blue light because it sedates the hens and increases their egg-laying.

Yes, society has learned many lessons, which I have tried to gather, and organize, and present to you in one book. A new way of life using color lies before you. The power of color keeps your biological clock ticking in harmony so that energy loss remains at a minimum and body metabolism flourishes for the promotion of youth extension. The application of color principles, therefore, offers you prolongevity and an improvement in the quality of living.

Resources for More Information

ASSOCIATIONS

American College of Advancement in Medicine
23121 Verdugo Drive
Suite 204
Laguna Hills, CA 92653
Telephone: (714) 583-7666 (inside California)
(800) 532-3688 (outside California)
Executive Director: Edward A. Shaw, Ph.D.

Great Lakes Association of Clinical Medicine
70 West Huron Street
Chicago, IL 60610
Telephone: (312) 266-7246
Executive Director: Jack Hank

EQUIPMENT

William C. Douglass, M.D.
Medical Image Marketing
P.O. Box 1568
Clayton, GA 30525
Telephone: (800) 227-6269

Network
25 West Fairview Avenue
Dover, NJ 07801
Telephone: (800) 777-4636
Proprietor: Dan Kassell

Pure Health Concepts
2430 Herodian Way
Suite 280
Smyrna, GA 30080
Telephone: (404) 859-9040 (telephone)
(404) 264-6179 (voice mail)

LITERATURE

Cancer Control Society
2043 North Berendo Street
Los Angeles, CA 90027
Telephone: (213) 663-7801
Executive Secretary: Lorraine Rosenthal

This organization has two items available that describe in detail the work of John Ott:

1. A "John Ott issue" of the Cancer Control Society jour-

nal, which also includes a list of other sources in the United States for full-spectrum, radiation-shielded Ott-Lite fluorescent light fixtures. The issue costs $5.

2. A complete update in journal form of John Ott's most current work (four articles), reprinted from *The International Journal of Biosocial Research*. Each paper costs $5.

TECHNIQUES

Helen Irlen, President
The Irlen Institute
5380 Village Road
Long Beach, CA 90808
Telephone: (213) 496-2550

Russell Jaffe, M.D., Ph.D.
Princeton Biocenter and Health
  Studies Collegium
862 Route 518
Skilman, NJ 08558
Telephone: (609) 924-8607

Suggested Additional Reading

Abbott, Arthur G. *The Color of Life*. New York: McGraw-Hill Book Co., 1947.

Amber, R. B. *Color Therapy*. Calcutta, India: Firma KLM Private, Ltd., 1976.

Anderson, Mary. *Colour Healing*. New York: Samuel Weiser, Inc., 1975.

Andrews, Donald Hatch. *The Symphony of Life*. Lee's Summit, MO: Unity Books, 1966.

Avery, Kevin Quinn. *The Numbers of Life*. New York: Freeway Press, 1974.

Babbitt, Edwin S. *The Principles of Light and Color*. New Hyde Park, NY: University Books, 1967.

Bailey, Alice A. *Esoteric Psychology*, Vol. I. New York: Lucis Publishing Co., 1936.

Basford, Leslie, and Joan Pick. *The Rays of Light*. London: Sampson Low, Marston and Co., 1966.

Beesley, R. P. *The Robe of Many Colours*. Lewes, Sussex, England: The College of Psycho-therapeutics, 1953.

Birren, Faber. *Color in Your World*. New York: Collier Books, 1962.

Birren, Faber. *Color Psychology and Color Therapy*. Secaucus, NJ: University Books, 1961.

Birren, Faber. "The Effects of Color on the Human Organism," *American Journal of Occupational Therapy* (1959).

Birren, Faber. *History of Color in Painting*. New York: Reinhold Publishing Corp., 1965.

Birren, Faber. *New Horizons in Color*. New York: Reinhold Publishing Corp., 1955.

Boos-Hamburger, Hilde. *The Creative Power of Colour*. London: The Michael Press, 1973.

Bragg, Sir William. *The Universe of Light*. New York: Dover Publications, Inc., 1959.

Burgoyne, Thomas H. *The Light of Egypt*, Vol. 1. Denver: Astro Philosophical Publishing Co., 1963.

Campbell, Florence. *Your Days Are Numbered*. Ferndale, PA: The Gateway, 1975.

Cheasley, Clifford, W. *Numerology*. Mokelumne Hill, CA: Health Research, 1972.

Cheasley, Clifford W. *What's in Your Name?* Mokelumne Hill, CA: Health Research, 1968.

Chevreul, M. D. *The Principles of Harmony and Contrast of Colours*. London: Bell & Daldy, 1870.

Collin, Rodney. *The Theory of Celestial Influence*. New York: Samuel Weiser, Inc., 1975.

Color. New York: Time-Life Books, 1970.

Color Healing. Mokelumne Hill, CA: Health Research, 1965.

Curtiss, Harriette Augusta, and F. Homer Curtiss. *The Message of Aquaria*. Washington, DC: The Curtiss Philosophic Book Co., 1938.

Curtiss, Harriette Augusta, and F. Homer Curtiss. *The Voice of Isis*. Washington, DC: The Curtiss Philosophic Book Co., 1926.

David, William. *The Harmonics of Sound, Color & Vibration*. Marina del Rey, CA: DeVorss & Co., 1980.

DeBary, William Theodore (general editor). *Sources of Indian Tradition*, Vol. I. New York: Columbia University Press, 1958.

Desautels, Paul E. *The Gem Kingdom*. New York: Random House, 1977.

Diamantidis, Spiro A. *Chromatics: Be the Best with Colour*. Athens, Greece: Paralax, 1990.

Don, Frank. *Color Your World*. New York: Destiny Books, 1977.

Edelson, Richard. "Treatment of Cutaneous T-Cell Lymphoma by Extracorporeal Photochemotherapy," *New England Journal of Medicine* (Feb. 5, 1987).

Eeman, L. E. *The Technique of Conscious Evolution*. Ashingdon, England: The C. W. Daniel Co., Ltd., 1948.

Evans, Ralph M. *An Introduction to Color*. New York: John Wiley & Sons, Inc., 1948.

Faber, William J., and Morton Walker. *Pain, Pain Go Away*. Mountain View, CA: Ishi Press International, 1990.

Fabri, Ralph. *Color: A Complete Guide for Artists*. New York: Watson-Guptill Publications, 1967.

Fletcher, John (editor). *Goethe's Approach to Colour* (translated by Hilde Boos-Hamburger). London: The Michael Press, 1958.

Goethe, Johann Wolfgang von. *Theory of Colours* (translated by Charles Lock Eastlake). Cambridge, MA: The M.I.T. Press, 1970.

Graves, Maitland. *The Art of Color and Design*. New York: McGraw-Hill Book Co., 1941.

Graves, Maitland. *Fundamentals*. New York: McGraw-Hill Book Co., 1952.

Guptill, Arthur L. *Color in Sketching and Rendering*. New York: Reinhold Publishing Corp., 1935.

Guptill, Arthur L. *Color Manual for Artists*. New York: Reinhold Publishing Corp., 1946.

Hall, Manly P. *Man, the Grand Symbol of the Mysteries*. Los Angeles: The Philosophical Research Society, 1972.

Halpern, Steven. *Tuning the Human Instrument*. Belmont, CA: Spectrum Research Institute, 1978.

Halpern, Steven, and Louis Savary. *Sound Health: The Music and Sounds that Make Us Whole.* San Francisco: Harper & Row, 1985.

Heline, Corinne. *Color and Music in the New Age.* La Canada, CA: New Age Press, Inc., 1964.

Hills, Christopher. *Nuclear Evolution: Discovery of the Rainbow Body.* Boulder Creek, CA: University of the Trees Press, 1979.

Hills, Christopher. *Rise of the Phoenix.* Boulder Creek, CA: Common Ownership Press, 1979.

Hodges, Doris M. *Healing Stones.* Perry, IA: Pyramid Publishers of Iowa, 1961.

Hunt, Roland T. *The Eighth Key to Colour.* London: L. N. Fowler & Co., Ltd., 1965.

Hunt, Roland T. *Fragrant and Radiant Healing Symphony.* London: L. N. Fowler & Co., Ltd., 1937.

Hunt, Roland T. *The Seven Keys to Colour Healing.* Ashingdon, England: The C. W. Daniel Co., Ltd., 1963.

Jacobson, Egbert. *Basic Color.* Chicago: Paul Theobald, 1948.

Johnson, Kendall. *The Living Aura: Radiation Field Photography and the Kirlian Effect.* New York: Hawthorn Books, Inc., 1975.

Jordan, Juno. *Numerology: The Romance in Your Name.* Santa Barbara, CA: J. F. Rowny Press, 1965.

Kandinsky, Wassily. *The Art of Spiritual Harmony.* Boston: Houghton Mifflin Co., 1914.

Kargere, Audrey. *Color & Personality.* York Beach, ME: Samuel Weiser, Inc., 1982.

Katz, David. *The World of Color.* London: Kegan Paul, Trench, Trubner & Co., 1935.

Kilner, Walter J. *The Aura.* New York: Samuel Weiser, Inc., 1973.

Klein, Adrian Bernard. *Colour-Music.* London: Lockwood & Son, 1930.

Kruger, Helen. *Other Healers, Other Cures.* New York: Bobbs-Merrill Co., Inc., 1974.

Kunz, George Frederick. *The Curious Lore of Precious Stones.* New York: Dover Publications, Inc., 1971.

Ladd-Franklin, Christine. *Colour and Colour Theories.* New York: Harcourt, Brace & Co., 1929.

Lakhovsky, Georges. *The Secrets of Life* (translated by Mark Clement). Stockwell, England: True Health Publishing Co., 1951.

Loynes, Jesse. *Colour Dynamics.* London: Jesse Loynes, 1976.

Luckiesh, Matthew. *Color and Colors.* New York: D. Van Nostrand Co., Inc., 1938.

Luckiesh, Matthew. *Color and Its Applications.* New York: D. Van Nostrand Co., Inc., 1921.

Luscher, Max. *The Luscher Color Test* (translated and edited by Ian Scott). New York: Pocket Books, 1971.

MacIvor, Virginia, and Sandra LaForest. *Vibrations.* New York: Samuel Weiser, Inc., 1979.

Maerz, A., and M. R. Paul. *A Dictionary of Color.* New York: McGraw-Hill Book Co., 1930.

Marcum, David. *The Dow Jones-Irwin Guide to Fine Gems and Jewelry.* Homewood, IL: Dow Jones-Irwin, 1986.

Mayer, Gladys. *Colour and Healing.* Sussex, England: New Knowledge Books, 1960.

Munsell, Albert H. *A Color Notation.* Baltimore, MD: Munsell Color Co., 1936.

Munsell, Albert H. *Munsell Book of Color.* Baltimore, MD: Munsell Color Co., 1929.

Ostwald, Wilhelm. *Colour Science.* London: Winsor & Newton, Ltd., 1931.

Ott, John. "Color and Light: Their Effects on Plants, Animals and People," *International Journal of Biosocial Research,* special subject issues (1985–1988).

Ouseley, S.G.J. *The Power of the Rays.* London: L. N. Fowler & Co., Ltd., 1951.

Parry, Barbara L., Norman E. Rosenthal, Lawrence Tamarkin, and Thomas A. Wehr. "Treatment of a Patient with Seasonal Premenstrual Syndrome," *American Journal of Psychiatry* (June 1987).

Raleigh, A. S. *Hermetic Science of Motion and Number.* Chicago: George W. Wiggs, 1924.

Ramacharaka, Yogi. *Fourteen Lessons in Yogi Philosophy.* Chicago: Yoga Publication Society, 1931.

Ramadahn. *Colour and Healing for the New Age.* London: Ursula Roberts, 1954.

Reichenbach, Hans. *Atom and Cosmos* (translated by Edward S. Allen). New York: Macmillan Co., 1933.

Renner, Paul. *Order and Harmony* (translated by Alexander Nesbitt). New York: Reinhold Publishing Corp., 1964.

Retallack, Dorothy. *The Sound and Music of Plants.* Marina del Rey, CA: DeVorss & Co., 1973.

Sander, C. G. *Colour in Health and Disease.* London: The C. W. Daniel Co., Ltd., 1926.

Sargent, Walter. *The Enjoyment and Use of Color.* New York: Charles Scribner's Sons, 1923.

Schindler, Maria. *Goethe's Theory of Colour.* Sussex, England: New Knowledge Books, 1964.

Shroeder, Lynn, and Sheilah Ostrander. *Psychic Discoveries Behind the Iron Curtain.* Englewood Cliffs, NJ: Prentice-Hall, 1970.

Silbey, Uma. *The Complete Crystal Guidebook.* San Francisco: U-read Publications, 1986.

Snow, William Benham. *The Therapeutics of Radiant Light and Heat and Convective Heat.* New York: Scientific Authors Publishing Co., 1909.

Steiner, Rudolf. *Colour.* London: Rudolf Steiner Press, 1935.

Stevens, Ernest J. *Lights, Colors, Tones and Nature's Finer Forces.* Mokelumne Hill, CA: Health Research, 1974.

Stevens, Ernest J. *Rhythms and Colors.* San Francisco: The Rainbow Publishers, 1938.

Sturzaker, Doreen and James. *Colour and the Kabalah.* New York: Samuel Weiser, Inc., 1975.

Taylor, Ariel Yvon, and H. Warren Hyer. *Numerology—Its Facts and Secrets.* New York: C & R Anthony, Inc., 1956.

Valla, Mary. *The Power of Numbers.* Santa Monica, CA: DeVorss & Co., 1971.

Wagner, Carlton. *The Wagner Color Response*. Santa Barbara, CA: Wagner Institute for Color Research, 1985.

Wehr, Thomas A., et al. "Eye Versus Skin Phototherapy of Seasonal Affective Disorder," *American Journal of Psychiatry* (June 1987).

Weizsacker, C. F. von, and J. Juilfs. *Contemporary Physics* (translated by Arnold J. Pomerans). New York: George Braziller, 1982.

Wilson, Annie, and Lilla Bek. *What Colour Are You?* Wellingborough, Northamptonshire, England: Turnstone Press Ltd., 1981.

Winston, Shirley Rabb. *Music as the Bridge*. Virginia Beach, VA: A.R.E. Press, 1972.

Wright, W. D. *The Measurement of Colour*. London: Adam Hilger, Ltd., 1944.

Wright, W. D. *The Rays Are Not Coloured*. London: Adam Hilger, Ltd., 1967.

Index